THE LEAVING

STORIES BY
BUDGE WILSON

Stoddart

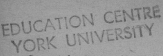
Copyright © 1990 by Budge Wilson

This paperback edition published in 1992 by
Stoddart Publishing Co. Limited
34 Lesmill Road
Toronto, Canada
M3B 2T6

Reprinted in May 1993

Hardcover edition published in 1990, and trade paperback edition in 1991, by House of Anansi Press Limited.

Canadian Cataloguing in Publication Data

Wilson, Budge
      The leaving

ISBN 0-7736-7363-6

I. Title.

PS8595.I57L4 1992   C813'.54   C92-093230-4
PR9199.3.W55L4 1992

Cover Painting: Christopher Pratt.
Typesetting: Tony Gordon Ltd.
Printed and bound in United States of America

The author wishes to thank The Canada Council and the Ontario Arts Council for assistance in the writing of this book.

Contents

The stories in this collection have been published previously
as follows:

"The Metaphor" in *Chatelaine* and *Inside Stories II*

"The Diary" in *Herizons*

"Mr. Manuel Jenkins" in *Dinosaur Review*

"Lysandra's Poem" in *Antigonish Review*

"The Leaving" in *Atlantis*

"The Reunion" in *The Toronto Star*

"Waiting" in the *University of Windsor Review*, *The Journey
Prize Anthology*, and *The One You Call Sister*

To my husband,
Alan

Enfin, Alain

THE
METAPHOR

Miss Hancock was plump and unmarried and over-enthusiastic. She was fond of peasant blouses encrusted with embroidery, from which loose threads invariably dangled. Like a heavy bird, she fluttered and flitted from desk to desk, inspecting notebooks, making suggestions, dispensing eager praise. Miss Hancock was our teacher of literature and creative writing.

If one tired of scrutinizing Miss Hancock's clothes, which were nearly always as flamboyant as her nature, one could still contemplate her face with considerable satisfaction. It was clear that this was a face that had once been pretty, although cloakroom discussions of her age never resulted in any firm conclusions. In any case, by now it was too late for simple, unadorned prettiness. What time had taken away from her, Miss Hancock tried to replace by artificial means, and she applied her makeup with an excess of zeal and a minimum of control. Her face was truly amazing. She was fond of luminous frosted lipsticks — in hot pink, or something closer to purple or magenta. Her eyelashes curled up and out singly, like a row of tiny bent sticks. Surrounding her eyes, the modulations of colour, toners, shadows could keep a student interested for half an hour if he or she were bored with a grammar assignment. Her head was covered with a profusion of small busy curls, which were brightly, aggressively golden — "in bad taste," my mother said, "like the rest of her."

However, do not misunderstand me. We were fond of Miss

Hancock. In fact, almost to a person, we loved her. Our class, like most groups that are together for long periods of time, had developed a definite personality. By some fluke of geography or biology or school administration, ours was a cohesive group composed of remarkably backward grade 7 pupils — backward in that we had not yet embraced sophistication, boredom, cruelty, drugs, alcohol, or sex. Those who did not fit into our mould were in the minority and made little mark upon us. We were free to respond positively to Miss Hancock's literary excesses without fear of the mockery of our peers, and with an open and uninhibited delight that is often hard to find in any classroom above the level of grade 5. So Miss Hancock was able to survive, even to flourish, in our unique, sheltered environment.

Miss Hancock was equally at home in her two fields of creative writing and literature. It was the first time I had been excited, genuinely moved, by poems, plays, stories. She could analyze without destroying a piece of literature, and we argued about meanings and methods and creative intentions with passionate caring. She had a beautiful deeply modulated voice, and when she read poetry aloud, we sat bewitched, transformed. We could not have said which we loved best, Miss Hancock or her subject. They were all of a piece.

But it was in the area of composition, in her creative writing class, that Miss Hancock made the deepest mark upon me. She had that gift of making most of us want to write, to communicate, to make a blank sheet of paper into a beautiful or at least an interesting thing. We were as drugged by words as some children are by electronic games.

One October day, just after Thanksgiving, Miss Hancock came into the classroom and faced us, eyes aglitter, hands clasped in front of her embroidered breasts.

"Today," she announced, clapping her dimpled hands together, her charm bracelets jingling, "we are going to do a lovely exercise. Such *fun*!" She lifted her astonishing eyes to the classroom ceiling. "A whole new world of composition is about to open for you in one glorious *whoosh*." She stood there, arms now raised, elbows bent, palms facing us, enjoying her dramatic pause. "After today," she announced in a loud confidential whisper, "you will have a brand-new weapon in your arsenal of writing skills. You will possess . . . (pause again) The Metaphor!" Her arms fell, and she clicked to the blackboard in her patent-leather pumps to start the lesson. Her dazzling curls shone in the afternoon sunlight and jiggled as she wrote. Then, with a board full of examples and suggestions, she began her impassioned discourse on The Metaphor. I listened, entranced. Miss Hancock may have been in poor taste, but at that time in my life she was my entry to something I did not yet fully understand but that I knew I wanted.

"And now," Miss Hancock announced, after the lucid and fervent presentation of her subject, "The Metaphor is yours — to *use*, to *enjoy*, to *relish*." She stood poised, savouring one of her breathless pauses. "I now want you to take out your notebooks," she continued, "and make a list. Write down the members of your family, your home, your pets, anything about which you feel *deeply*. Then," she went on, "I want you to describe everyone and everything on your list with a pungent and a telling metaphor." She gave a little clap. "Now *start*!" she cried. She sat down at her desk, clasping her hands together so tightly that the knuckles looked polished. Smiling tensely, frilled eyes shining, she waited.

All but the dullest of us were excited. This was an unfamiliar way of looking at things. Better still, it was a brand-new method of talking about them.

Miss Hancock interrupted us just one more time. "Write quickly," she urged from her glowing, expectant position at the desk. "Don't think too hard. Let your writing, your words, emerge from you like a mysterious and elegant blossom. Let it all *out*" — she closed her lacy eyes — "without restraint, without inhibition, with *verve*."

Well, we did. The results, when we read them out to her, were, as one might expect, hackneyed, undistinguished, ordinary. But we were delighted with ourselves. And she with us. She wrote our metaphors on the blackboard and expressed her pleasure with small, delighted gasping sounds.

"My dog is a clown in a spotted suit."

"My little brother George is a whirling top."

"The spruce tree was a tall lady in a stiff dress."

"My dad is a warm wood stove."

And so it went. Finally it was my turn. I offered metaphors for my father, my grandmother, my best friend, the waves at Peggy's Cove. Then I looked at the metaphor for my mother. I had not realized I had written so much.

"Miss Hancock," I hesitated, "the one for my mother is awfully long. You probably don't want to write all this stuff down."

"Oh, *heavens*, Charlotte," breathed Miss Hancock, "of *course* I want it! Read it all to us. Do, Charlotte. Oh, *do*!"

I began: "My mother is a flawless modern building, created of glass and the smoothest of pale concrete. Inside are business offices furnished with beige carpets and gleaming chromium. In every room there are machines — telex machines, mimeograph machines, and sleek typewriters. They are buzzing and clicking away, absorbing and spitting out information with a speed and skill that is not normal. Downstairs, at ground level, people walk in and out, tracking mud and dirt over the steel-grey tiles, marring the cool perfection of the building. There are no comfortable chairs in the lobby."

I sat down, eyes on my desk. There was a pause so long that I finally felt forced to look up. Miss Hancock was standing there at the front of the room, chalk poised, perfectly still. Then she turned around quickly and wrote the whole metaphor verbatim (verbatim!) on the board. When she faced us again, she looked normal once more. Smiling brightly, she said, "Very, *very* good, class! I had planned to discuss with you what you all *meant* by your metaphors; I had hoped to probe their *significance*. But I have to leave early today because of a dental appointment." Then, with five vigorous sweeps of her blackboard eraser, the whole enticing parade of metaphors disappeared from the board, leaving us feeling vaguely deprived. It also left me feeling more than vaguely relieved. "Class dismissed!" said Miss Hancock cheerily, and then, "Charlotte. May I see you for a moment before you go."

When the others had gathered up their books and their leftover lunches, they disappeared into the corridor. I went up to the front of the room to Miss Hancock's desk. She was sitting there soberly, hands still, eyes quiet.

"Yes, Miss Hancock?" I inquired, mystified.

"Charlotte," she began, "your metaphors were unusually good, unusually interesting. For someone your age, you have quite a complex vocabulary, a truly promising way of expressing yourself."

Ah. So this was why she wanted to see me. But apparently it was not.

"I wonder," she continued slowly, carefully, "do you have anything you would like to discuss about your mother's metaphor?"

I thought about that.

"No," I replied. "I don't think so. I don't really know what it means. It just sort of came out. I feel kind of funny about it."

"Lots of things just sort of come out when you're writing," said Miss Hancock quietly, oh so quietly, as though she were afraid something fragile might break if she spoke too quickly, too loudly. "And there's no need to feel funny about it. I don't want to push you even a little bit, but are you really sure you don't want to discuss it?" I could tell that she was feeling concerned and kind, not nosy.

"Lookit," I said, using an expression that my mother particularly disliked, "that's really nice of you, but I can't think of anything at all to say. Besides, even though you say there's no need to feel funny, I really do feel sort of creepy about it. And I'm not all that crazy about the feeling." I paused, not sure of what else to say.

Miss Hancock was suddenly her old self again. "*Well!*" she said cheerfully, as she rose. "That's perfectly fine. I just wanted you to know that your writing was very intriguing today, and that it showed a certain maturity that surprised and delighted me." She gathered up her books, her purse, her pink angora cardigan, and started off toward the corridor. At the door, she stopped and turned around, solemn and quiet once more. "Charlotte," she said, "if you ever need any help — with your writing, or, well, with any other kind of problem — just let me know." Then she turned abruptly and clicked off in the direction of the staff room, waving her hand in a fluttery farewell. "My dental appointment," she called merrily.

I walked home slowly, hugging my books to my chest. The mid-October sun shone down upon the coloured leaves that littered the sidewalk, and I kicked and shuffled as I walked, enjoying the swish and scrunch, savouring the sad-sweet feeling of doom that October always gives me. I thought for a while about my metaphor — the one Miss Hancock had asked about — and then I decided to push it out of my head.

When I arrived home, I opened the door with my key, entered the front porch, took off my shoes, and read the note on the hall table. It was written in flawless script on a small piece of bond paper. It said: "At a Children's Aid board meeting. Home by 5. Please tidy your room."

The hall table was polished, antique, perfect. It contained one silver salver for messages and a small ebony lamp with a white shade. The floor of the entrance hall was tiled. The black and white tiles shone in the sunlight, unmarked by any sign of human contact. I walked over them carefully, slowly, having slipped and fallen once too often.

Hunger. I went into the kitchen and surveyed it thoughtfully. More black and white tiles dazzled the eye, and the cupboards and walls were a blinding spotless white. The counters shone, empty of jars, leftovers, canisters, appliances. The whole room looked as though it were waiting for the movers to arrive with the furniture and dishes. I made myself a peanut-butter sandwich, washed the knife and plate, and put everything away. Then I went upstairs to my room, walking up the grey stair carpet beside the off-white walls, glancing absently at the single lithograph in its black frame. "My home," I said aloud, "is a box. It is cool and quiet and empty and uninteresting. Nobody lives in the box." Entering my room, I looked around. A few magazines were piled on the floor beside my bed. On my dresser, a T-shirt lay on top of my ivory brush and comb set. Two or three books were scattered over the top of my desk. I picked up the magazines, removed the T-shirt, and put the books back in the bookcase. There. Done.

Then I called Julia Parsons, who was my best friend, and went over to her house to talk about boys. When I returned at six o'clock, my mother, who had been home only one hour, had prepared a complicated three-course meal — expert, delicious, nutritious. "There's food in the box," I mused.

Since no one else had much to say at dinner, I talked about school. I told them about Miss Hancock's lesson on The Metaphor. I said what a marvellous teacher she was, how even the dumbest of us had learned to enjoy writing compositions, how she could make the poetry in our textbook so exciting to read and to hear.

My father listened attentively, enjoying my enthusiasm. He was not a lively or an original man, but he was an intelligent person who liked to watch eagerness in others. "You're very fortunate, Charlotte," he said, "to find a teacher who can wake you up and make you love literature."

"Is she that brassy Miss Hancock whom I met at the home and school meeting?" asked my mother.

"What do you mean, brassy?"

"Oh. You know. Overdone, too much enthusiasm. Flamboyant. Orange hair. Is she the one?"

"Yes," I said.

"Oh," said my mother, without emphasis of any kind. "Her. Charlotte, would you please remove the dishes and bring in the dessert. Snow pudding. In the fridge, top left-hand side. Thank you."

That night I lay in the bath among the Estée Lauder bubbles (gift from my father on my last birthday) and created metaphors. I loved baths. The only thing nicer than one bath a day was two. Julia said that if I kept taking so many baths, my skin would get dry and crisp, and that I would be wrinkled before I was thirty. That was too far away to worry about. She also said that taking baths was disgusting and that showers were more hygienic. She pointed out that I was soaking in my own dirt, like bathers in the fetid Ganges. I thought this a bit excessive and said so. "For pete's sake!" I exclaimed. "If I have two baths a day, I can't be sitting in very much dirt. Besides, it's *therapeutic*."

"It's *what*?"

"Therapeutic. Water play. I read about it in *Reader's Digest* at the doctor's office. They let kids play with water when they're wild and upset. And now they're using warm baths to soothe the patients in mental hospitals."

"So?"

"So it could be useful if I happen to end up crazy." I laughed. I figured that would stop her. It did.

In the bath I always did a lot of things besides wash. I lifted up mounds of the tiny bubbles and held them against the fluorescent light over the sink. The patterns and shapes were delicate, like minute filaments of finest lace. I poked my toes through the bubbles and waved their hot pinkness to and fro among the static white waves. I hopefully examined my breasts for signs of sudden growth. If I lay down in the tub and brought the bubbles up over my body and squeezed my chest together by pressing my arms inward, I could convince myself that I was full-breasted and seductive. I did exercises to lengthen my hamstrings, in order to improve my splits for the gymnastics team. I thought about Charles Swinimer. I quoted poetry out loud with excessive feeling and dramatic emphasis, waving my soapy arms around and pressing my eloquent hand against my flat chest. And from now on, I also lay there and made up metaphors, most of them about my mother.

"My mother is a white picket fence — straight, level. The fence stands in a field full of weeds. The field is bounded on all sides by thorny bushes and barbed wire."

"My mother is a lofty mountain capped by virgin snow. The air around the mountain is clear and clean and very cold." I turned on more hot water. "At the base of the mountain grow gnarled and crooked trees, surrounded by scrub brush and poison ivy."

Upon leaving the bath, I would feel no wiser. Then I would clean the tub very carefully indeed. It was necessary.

Not, mind you, that my mother ranted and raved about her cleanliness. Ranting and raving were not part of her style. "I know you will agree," she would say very oh ever so sweetly, implying in some oblique way that I certainly did not agree, "that it is an inconsiderate and really ugly thing to leave a dirty tub." Then she would lead me with a subtle soft-firm pressure into the bathroom so that we might inspect together a bathtub ringed with sludge, sprinkled with hair and dried suds. "Not," she would say quietly, "a very pretty sight."

And what, I would ask myself, is so terrible about that? Other mothers — I know; I had heard them — nagged, yelled, scolded, did terrible and noisy things. But what was it about my mother's methods that left me feeling so depraved, so unsalvageable?

But of course I was thirteen by now, and knew all about cleaning tubs and wiping off countertops and sweeping up crumbs. A very small child must have been a terrible test to that cool and orderly spirit. I remember those days. A toy ceased to be a toy and began to be a mess the moment it left the toy cupboard. "I'm sure," she would say evenly, "that you don't want to have those blocks all over the carpet. Why not keep them all in one spot, over there behind Daddy's chair?" From time to time I attempted argument.

"But Mother, I'm making a garden."

"Then make a *little* garden. They're every bit as satisfying as large, sprawling unmanageable farms."

And since no one who was a truly nice person would want a large, sprawling unmanageable farm, I would move my blocks behind the chair and make my small garden there. Outside, our backyard was composed of grass and flowers, plus one evergreen tree that dropped neither fuzzy buds in the spring nor ragged leaves in the fall. No swing set made brown spots on that perfect lawn, nor was there a sandbox. Cats were known to use sandboxes as community toilets. Or so my mother told me. I assume she used the term *toilet* (a word not normally part of her vocabulary) instead of washroom, lest there be any confusion as to her meaning.

But in grade 7, you no longer needed a sandbox. My friends marvelled when they came to visit, which was not often. How serene my mother seemed, how lovely to look at, with her dark-blond hair, her flawless figure, her smooth hands. She never acted frazzled or rushed or angry, and her forehead was unmarked by age or worry lines. Her hair always looked as though a hairdresser had arrived at six o'clock to ready her for the day. "Such a peaceful house," my friends would say, clearly impressed, "and no one arguing or fighting." Then they would leave and go somewhere else for their snacks, their music, their hanging around.

No indeed, I thought. No fights in this house. It would be like trying to down an angel with a BB gun — both sacrilegious and futile. My father, thin and nervous, was careful about hanging up his clothes and keeping his sweaters in neat piles. He certainly did not fight with my mother. In fact, he said very little to her at all. He had probably learned early that to complain is weak, to rejoice is childish, to laugh is noisy. And moving around raises dust.

This civilized, this clean, this disciplined woman who was and is my mother, was also, if one were to believe her admirers, the mainstay of the community, the rock upon which the town was built. She chaired committees, ran bazaars, sat on boards. When I first heard about this, I thought it a very exciting thing that she sat on boards. If my mother, who sat so correctly on the needlepoint chair with her nylon knees pressed so firmly together, could actually sit on *boards*, there might be a rugged and reckless side to her that I had not yet met. The telephone rang constantly, and her softly controlled voice could be heard, hour after hour, arranging and steering and manipulating the affairs of the town.

Perhaps because she juggled her community jobs, her house-work, her cooking and her grooming with such quiet, calm efficiency, she felt scorn for those less able to cope. "Mrs. Langstreth says she is too *tired* to take on a table at the bazaar," she might say. It was not hard to imagine Mrs. Langstreth lounging on a sofa, probably in a turquoise chenille dressing gown, surrounded by full ashtrays and neglected children. Or my mother might comment quietly, but with unmistakable emphasis, "Gillian Munroe is having trouble with her children. And in my opinion, she has only herself to blame." The implication seemed to be that if Gillian Munroe's children were left in my mother's care for a few weeks, she could make them all into a perfectly behaved family. Which was probably true.

Certainly in those days I was well behaved. I spoke quietly, never complained, ate whatever was put before me, and obeyed all rules without question or argument. I was probably not even very unhappy, though I enjoyed weekdays much more than weekends. Weekends did not yet include parties or boys. It is true that Julia and I spent a lot of our time together talking about boys. I also remember stationing myself on the fence of the vacant lot on Seymour Street at five o'clock, the hour when Charles Swinimer could be expected to return from high school. As he passed, I would be too absorbed in my own activity to look at him directly. I would be chipping the bark off the fence, or reading, or pulling petals from a daisy — he loves me, he loves me not. Out of the corner of my eye, I feasted upon his jaw line, his confident walk, his shoulders. On the rare days when he would toss me a careless "Hi" (crumbs to a pigeon), I would have to dig my nails into the wood to keep from falling off, from fainting dead away. But that was the extent of my thrills. No boys had yet materialized in the flesh to offer themselves to me. Whatever else they were looking for, it was not acne, straight, brown stringy hair or measurements of 32-32-32.

So weekdays were still best. Weekdays meant school and particularly English class, where Miss Hancock delivered up feasts of succulent literature for our daily consumption. *Hamlet* was the thing that spring, the spring before we moved into junior high. So were a number of poems that left me weak and changed. And our composition class gathered force, filling us with a creative confidence that was heady stuff. We wrote short stories, played with similes, created poems that did and did not rhyme, felt we were capable of anything and everything; if Shakespeare, if Wordsworth, could do it, why couldn't we? Over it all, Miss Hancock presided, hands fluttering, voice atremble with a raw emotion.

But *Hamlet* dominated our literature classes from April to June. Like all serious students, we agonized and argued over its meaning, Hamlet's true intent, his sanity, his goal. Armed with rulers, we fought the final duel with its bloody sequence, and a four-foot Fortinbras stepped among the dead bodies between the desks to proclaim the ultimate significance of it all. At the end, Miss Hancock stood, hands clasped, knuckles white, tears standing in her eyes. And I cannot pretend that all of ours were dry.

At the close of the year, our class bought an enormous tasteless card of thanks and affixed it to a huge trophy. The trophy was composed of two brass-coloured Ionic pillars that were topped by a near-naked athlete carrying a spiky wreath. On the plate below was inscribed: "For you and Hamlet with love. The grade 7 class. 1965."

When my mother saw it, she came close to losing her cool control.

"Who chose it?" she asked, tight-lipped.

"Horace Hannington," I answered. Oh, don't spoil it, don't spoil it.

"That explains it," she said, and mercifully that was all.

❖ ❖ ❖

Junior high school passed, and so did innocence and acne. Hair curled, makeup intact, I entered high school the year that Charles Swinimer left for university. But there would be other fish to fry. Outwardly blasé, single-minded, and sixteen, I came into my first grade 10 class with a mixture of intense apprehension and a burning unequivocal belief that high school could and would deliver up to me all of life's most precious gifts — the admiration of my peers, local fame, boys, social triumphs. During August of that year, my family had moved to another school district. I entered high school with a clean slate. It was terrifying to be so alone. I also knew that it was a rare and precious opportunity; I could approach life without being branded with my old failures, my old drawbacks. I was pretty; I had real curves; I was anonymous; I melted into the crowd. No one here would guess that I had once been such a skinny, pimply wretch.

Our first class was geography, and I knew enough of the material to be able to let my eyes and mind wander. Before the end of the period, I knew that the boy to pursue was Howard Oliver, that the most prominent and therefore the most potentially useful or dangerous girl was Gladys Simpson, that geography was uninteresting, that the teacher was strict. To this day I can smell the classroom during that first period — the dry and acrid smell of chalk, the cool, sweet fragrance of the freshly waxed floors, the perspiration that travelled back to me from Joey Elliot's desk.

The next period was English. My new self-centred and self-conscious sophistication had not blunted my love of literature, my desire to write, to play with words, to express my discoveries and confusions. I awaited the arrival of the teacher with masked but real enthusiasm. I was not prepared for the entrance of Miss Hancock.

Miss Hancock's marked success with fifteen years of grade 7 students had finally transported her to high places. She entered the classroom, wings spread, ready to fly. She was used to success, and she was eager to sample the pleasure of a group of older and more perceptive minds. Clad in royal blue velour, festooned with gold chains, hair glittering in the sun pouring in from the east window, fringed eyes darting, she faced the class, arms raised. She paused.

"Let us pray!" said a deep male voice from the back row. It was Howard Oliver. Laughter exploded in the room. Behind my Duo Tang folder, I snickered fiercely.

Miss Hancock's hands fluttered wildly. It was as though she were waving off an invasion of poisonous flies.

"Now, now, class!" she exclaimed with a mixture of tense jollity and clear panic. "We'll have none of *that*! Please turn to page seven in your textbook. I'll read the selection aloud to you first, and then we'll discuss it." She held the book high in the palm of one hand; the other was raised like an admonition, an artistic beckoning.

The reading was from Tennyson's "Ulysses." I had never heard it before. As I listened to her beautiful voice, the old magic took hold, and no amount of peer pressure could keep me from thrilling to the first four lines she read:

> "*I am a part of all that I have met;*
> *Yet all experience is an arch wherethro'*
> *Gleams that untravell'd world, whose margin fades*
> *For ever and for ever when I move.*"

But after that, it was difficult even to hear her. Guffaws sprang up here and there throughout the room. Gladys Simpson whispered something behind her hand to the girl beside her and then broke into fits of giggles. Paper airplanes flew. The wits of grade 10 offered comments: "Behold the Bard!" "Bliss! Oh, poetic bliss!" "Hancock! Whocock? Hancock! Hurray!" "Don't faint, class! *Don't faint!*"

I was caught in a stranglehold somewhere between shocked embarrassment and a terrible desire for concealment. No other members of the class shared my knowledge of Miss Hancock or my misery. But I knew I could not hide behind that Duo Tang folder forever.

It was in fact ten days later when Miss Hancock recognized me. It could not have been easy to connect the eager skinny fan of grade 7 with the cool and careful person I had become. And she would not have expected to find a friend in that particular classroom. By then, stripped of fifteen years of overblown confidence, she offered her material shyly, hesitantly, certain of rejection, of humiliation. When our eyes met in class, she did not rush up to me to claim alliance or allegiance. Her eyes merely held mine for a moment, slid off, and then periodically slid back. There was a desperate hope in them that I could hardly bear to witness. At the end of the period, I waited until everyone had gone before I walked toward her desk on the way to the corridor. Whatever was going to happen, I wanted to be sure that it would not be witnessed.

When I reached her, she was sitting quietly, hands folded on top of her lesson book. I was reminded of another day, another meeting. The details were blurred; but I knew I had seen this Miss Hancock before. She looked at me evenly and said quietly, simply, "Hello, Charlotte. How nice to see you."

I looked at her hands, the floor, the blackboard, anywhere but at those searching eyes. "Hello, Miss Hancock," I said.

"Still writing metaphors?" she asked with a tentative smile.

"Oh, I dunno," I replied. But I was. Nightly, in the bathtub. And I kept a notebook in which I wrote them all down.

"Your writing showed promise, Charlotte." Her eyes were quiet, pleading. "I hope you won't forget that."

Or anything else, I thought. Oh, Miss Hancock, let me go. Aloud I said, "French is next, and I'm late."

She looked directly into my eyes and held them for a moment. Then she spoke. "Go ahead, Charlotte. Don't let me keep you."

She did not try to reach me again. She taught, or tried to teach her classes, as though I were not there. Week after week, she entered the room white with tension and left it defeated. I did not tell a living soul that I had ever seen her before.

One late afternoon in March of that year, Miss Hancock stepped off the curb in front of the school and was killed instantly by a school bus.

The next day, I was offered this piece of news with that mixture of horror and delight that so often attends the delivery of terrible tidings. When I heard it, I felt as though my chest and throat were constricted by bands of dry ice. During assembly, the principal came forward and delivered a short announcement of the tragedy, peppered with little complimentary phrases: ". . . a teacher of distinction . . ." ". . . a generous colleague . . ." ". . . a tragic end to a promising career . . ." Howard Oliver was sitting beside me; he had been showing me flattering attention of late. As we got up to disperse for classes, he said, "Poor old Whocock Hancock.

Quoting poetry to the angels by now." He was no more surprised than I was when I slapped him full across his handsome face, before I ran down the aisle of the assembly room, up the long corridor of the first floor, down the steps, and out into the parking lot. Shaking with dry, unsatisfying sobs, I hurried home through the back streets of the town and let myself in by the back door.

"What on earth is wrong, Charlotte?" asked my mother when she saw my stricken look, my heaving shoulders. There was real concern in her face.

"Miss Hancock is dead," I whispered.

"Miss *who*? Charlotte, speak up please."

"Miss Hancock. She teaches — *taught* — us grade 10 English."

"You mean that same brassy creature from grade 7?"

I didn't answer. I was crying out loud, with the abandon of a preschooler or someone who is under the influence of drugs.

"Charlotte, do please blow your nose and try to get hold of yourself. I can't for the life of me see why you're so upset. You never even told us she was your teacher this year."

I was rocking back and forth on the kitchen chair, arms folded over my chest. My mother stood there erect, invulnerable. It crossed my mind that no grade 10 class would throw paper airplanes in any group that *she* chose to teach.

"Well, then," she said, "why or how did she die?"

I heard myself shriek, "I killed her! I killed her!"

Halting, gasping, I told her all of it. I described her discipline problems, the cruelty of the students, my own blatant betrayal.

"For goodness' sake, Charlotte," said my mother, quiet but clearly irritated, "don't lose perspective. She couldn't keep order, and she had only herself to blame." That phrase sounded familiar to me. "A woman like that can't survive for five minutes in the high schools of today. There was nothing you could have done."

I was silent. I could have *said something*. Like thank you for grade 7. Or yes, I still have fun with The Metaphor. Or once, just once in this entire year, I could have *smiled* at her.

My mother was speaking again. "There's a great deal of ice. It would be very easy to slip under a school bus. And she didn't strike me as the sort of person who would exercise any kind of sensible caution."

"Oh, dear God," I was whispering, "I wish she hadn't chosen a *school bus*."

I cried some more that day and excused myself from supper. I heard my father say, "I think I'll just go up and see if I can help." But my mother said, "Leave her alone, Arthur. She's sixteen years old. It's time she learned how to cope. She's acting like a hysterical child." My father did not appear. Betrayal, I thought, runs in the family.

The next day I stayed home from school. I kept having periods of uncontrollable weeping, and even my mother could not send me off in that condition. Once again I repeated to her, to my father, "I killed her. We all killed her. But especially me."

"Charlotte."

Oh, I knew that voice, that tone. So calm, so quiet, so able to silence me with one word. I stopped crying and curled up in a tight ball on the sofa.

"Charlotte. I know you will agree with what I'm going to say to you. There is no need to speak so extravagantly. A sure and perfect control is what separates the civilized from the uncivilized." She inspected her fingernails, pushing down the quick of her middle finger with her thumb. "If you would examine this whole perfectly natural situation with a modicum of rationality, you would see that she got exactly what she deserved."

I stared at her.

"Charlotte," she continued, "I'll have to ask you to stop this nonsense. You're disturbing the even tenor of our home."

I said nothing. With a sure and perfect control, I uncoiled myself from my fetal position on the sofa. I stood up and left the living room.

Upstairs in my bedroom I sat down before my desk. I took my pen out of the drawer and opened my notebook. Extravagantly, without a modicum of rationality, I began to write.

"Miss Hancock was a birthday cake," I wrote. "This cake was frosted by someone unschooled in the art of cake decoration. It was adorned with a profusion of white roses and lime-green leaves, which drooped and dribbled at the edges where the pastry tube had slipped. The frosting was of an intense peppermint flavour, too sweet, too strong. Inside, the cake had two layers — chocolate and vanilla. The chocolate was rich and soft and very delicious. No one who stopped to taste it could have failed to enjoy it. The vanilla was subtle and delicate; only those thoroughly familiar with cakes, only those with great sensitivity of taste, could have perceived its true fine flavour. Because it was a birthday cake, it was filled with party favours. If you stayed long enough at the party, you could amass quite a large collection of these treasures. If you kept them for many years, they would amaze you by turning into pure gold. Most children would have been delighted by this cake. Most grown-ups would have thrown it away after one brief glance at the frosting.

"I wish that the party wasn't over."

---------------- ❖ ----------------

THE
DIARY

January 1

Here it is, then. You said on Friday that if I found it
impossible to talk about it, I should try to write it all down.
You suggested that it was a good way to start the New Year —
like a resolution — something new and changing. You told me
not to worry about grammar or sentence structure, but just to
let it all pour out like a boil releasing its poisons. Its *pus*, in
fact — your word, not mine. This is not easy for me. Releasing
anything, that is. Or, to tell you the truth, to write anything
without checking to make sure it is correct, without erasing
any mistakes or signs of carelessness. My father said that
anything worth doing was worth doing well. Nonetheless, I
will try. Fortunately, you also said that I don't have to show the
diary to you. I don't expect that I will. I can't bear the kind of
disloyalty that washes family linen, soiled or otherwise, in
public and to strangers. Although of course you are not really
a stranger. But you know what I mean.

And I'm here alone. No one can see what I'm saying or how
I'm saying it. But that's the crazy part. Even when I'm alone,
maybe especially when I'm alone, I sit in judgement upon
myself. I am my own judge and jailer. Probably that's hackneyed; it may even be a quote. But I'm going to try not to worry
about that sort of thing. This is a diary, not a piece of literature.

I am fifty-five years old. I am married to a businessman who is successful and scrupulously honest. His name is Meredith Wentworth. I feel that the name has weight and dignity. He usually treats me with respect and with decency. We have two sons, both of them in their twenties. Their names are Gerald and Luther. They have always been well behaved and courteous, and they are now employed in their father's business. I have no daughters. Some people say that this is unfortunate, but I don't mind at all, because you never really miss something you have never had.

Tonight the boys are coming to dinner with their girlfriends. I must put the turkey in the oven before too long. Gerald's girl wears too much makeup; her clothes are invariably too tight, and her name is Samantha. Can you believe such a name? I've often seen them together downtown, but this is the first time he has brought her home. When they are together, they touch one another far too much. This worries me. Meredith is almost certain to disapprove. And she is not Luther's type either. His girl's name is Jane, and she is everything a parent could hope for in a daughter-in-law. I am hoping against hope that they will marry.

❖ ❖ ❖

January 3

I didn't write yesterday because I was too tired. You said I was not to force it, although you also advised me to write *something* each day, even if it was just to say how I felt.

I feel terrible.

That's mainly because of New Year's dinner. But that's not primarily what you want me to write about. You said to try to write about my childhood. All right. The least I can do, I suppose, is to make an effort.

When I think back to my childhood, the first image I see is my father. He was enormous. Or at least so he seemed. In snapshots, he appears to be about the same height as other men, but even with that visual evidence before me, I find this hard to believe. He was very dark, with a black beard — in the days before anyone had a beard, except possibly one's grandfather. He wore thick glasses, and his eyes were very fixed and piercing behind them. He was a Presbyterian minister. I can see him up there, huge and erect in his black robes, lifted far above us by his pulpit and by his purpose. His voice was deep and powerful, and very compelling.

"The wages of sin is death!" he would boom down at us from on high. With his voice, his bearing, it was easy to believe him. Then the hymns would follow, militantly urging virtue, or melodiously promising peace and joy to the sinless. I believed everything he said. It was not hard to do this. After all, he was my father. Besides, he looked exactly like God.

New Year's dinner was just dreadful. Samantha's neckline was so low that you could see the division between her breasts. Meredith was very controlled and was as polite to her as to Jane, who wore a beige cashmere dress — very suitable. But I could see him looking at Samantha's dangling earrings, her untidy mass of curly hair, her *chest*, and his eyes were like stones. Gerald looked cross and uncomfortable, although I think they were doing something with their feet under the table. Jane was perfect, of course, and tried to draw Samantha into the conversation; but none of her topics seemed to be in areas that interested Samantha. She mentioned Junior League activities, a recent trip to Europe, inflation, the Princess of Wales's children, a whole spectrum of subjects; but Samantha had almost nothing to say. She is quite pretty, or would be if she would comb her hair and do something about her clothes. I can't for the life of me understand why Gerald doesn't make her change. He calls her Sam, and when he looks at her — I will admit to you now on paper something that I could never tell you face to face — I am jealous. No man has ever looked at me that way — as though he were seeing a vision — something delectable, desirable, but sparked with grace. But it is the

tenderness that really eats into my heart, and fills me with an
envy as green as grass. I said that no one had ever looked at me
like that, but that's not strictly true. There was Jamie. I thought
about Jamie as I watched them. Then I tried to concentrate on
the turkey, on the preparation and serving of food. I couldn't
cope with all the conflicting things I was feeling, or with the
vibrations shooting back and forth across the table.

❖ ❖ ❖

January 4

I wrote a lot yesterday, so I needn't write as much today.

My father was the strong parent in our house. My mother
was small and mousy, and I can't remember her with anything
but grey hair. She wore housedresses out of Eaton's catalogue,
and no makeup. She did everything my father asked or told
her to do, and she never argued. I don't ever remember a fight
in our house. I was an only child. My father talked a lot. He
told us about how to behave, but he was even more eager to
discuss sin. He described the wicked people in the congregation and in the town, and the evil things they did. It never
occurred to me to like these people. Or rarely. Once I started
a friendship with a girl called Gertie Bowman and invited her
home one day to play. She was a lot of fun, and I loved her
laugh, which was a sort of joyful shriek. My father took me
aside afterwards and told me that her father drank too much,
that her mother was a "bad woman," and that it would be a
poor example for a minister's daughter to spend much time
with people like that. I could see his point. He also talked a
great deal about lying and stealing and coveting and cheating.
And vanity. One day my mother came home in a cornflower-
blue dress. She looked pretty, which was unusual for her, and
she seemed cheerful and happy. I was so proud of her, and
hugged her, and told her how lovely she looked. My father
stood up and said, "Where did you get the money?" and she

said, "From Aunt Julia, for Christmas." Then he said, "I find the colour vulgar, and besides, we could use the money. Even I can tell that that dress was not cheap. We are not royalty. We have no need of such finery." She said, "Yes, Arthur," and left the room. She looked small and tired, even from the back. We never saw the dress again.

I've written more than I intended.

❖ ❖ ❖

January 5

I wanted so badly to get to heaven when I was small. I still do. It sounded like such a peaceful shining place. I was scared of God, but I was assured by my father that if I did exactly what He told me to do, He would be kind and loving forever. This meant that I must never, *never* lie or steal or cheat or even think bad thoughts. It was particularly hard not to think bad thoughts, but every time one nudged itself into my head, I would order it out, clench my fists, and try to think of beautiful things. I became very skillful at this, but it took enormous effort.

I always kept hoping that if I did everything right, my father, like God, would also be soft and loving. Sometimes he said "Good for you, Allison" when I did something *unusually* wonderful, like the time I gave away my new doll to a poor girl on Water Street who had received no Christmas presents. It wasn't my idea, which I suppose would have been better, but at least I did it. But even then he didn't hug me or anything, or say "I love you," or stroke my hair the way I'd seen other fathers do. Dolls' heads were made of china then, with soft cloth bodies. She had blue eyes, just like real eyes, with eyelashes, and they opened and closed when you changed the position of her head. She had a mauve dress with ruffles on the skirt, and a headful of tiny black curls — real hair, not just painted on.

❖ ❖ ❖

January 6

I'm too tired today to write. Gerald came to see his father this morning, and they were in Meredith's study for twenty-five minutes. Although I couldn't hear what they were saying, I didn't like the sound of their voices. When they came out, Meredith was looking pale and frozen, but saying nothing. Gerald turned to his father and said, "I'm *twenty-six*, Dad!" with a look on his face that I can't even describe. Then he dashed out of the house, slamming the door, without even looking at me. Meredith stood perfectly still in the front hall, and then went back into his study, closing the door with exaggerated care.

I wish I didn't have this awful desire to cry all the time.

❖ ❖ ❖

January 7

When I saw you today, you said that I must try to write about the past, even if my mind is preoccupied with the present. It's all right, you said, to mention what's going on now, but that I might find everything, including the present, easier to cope with if I dug up all that really old stuff.

I forgot to mention that the day I gave away my doll, my mother cried. I can't remember if I did. I can't remember anything else at all about that day.

❖ ❖ ❖

January 8

"I will never, never forgive you if I ever catch you lying." That is exactly what my father said to me that day in June. I can hear him still, as clearly as if it were yesterday. He had seen a neighbouring boy, Joe Hamandi was his name, steal one of

ur daffodils the day before. The next day, when Joe appeared
n the sidewalk, Father rushed out to scold him, to punish him.
His face was red with anger, and his eyes were like black bullets.
"How dare you pick one of our flowers!" he shouted, waving
is fist. "How dare you steal my property!" The little boy was
white with fright. "I didn't! I didn't!" he whispered. "Someone
else did it! *I* didn't!" And then he ran away. "Liar! Liar!" yelled
my father. "Worse by far than a thief!" And then he told me
what he would do to me if he ever caught me lying.

Gerald wants to marry Samantha. We are all in a state of
shock. Jane and Luther won't even discuss it with him, and
Meredith, of course, is beside himself.

I don't know what to do. Worse still, I don't even know what
to think.

❖ ❖ ❖

January 9

This is a bad part, and will be hard for me to tell. But I don't
have to show it to you if I don't want to. You told me that.

One day when I was eight years old, Father was in a terrible
mood. It was Saturday, which meant that he was writing his
sermon, and he was always nervous on those days. I was playing
hopscotch on the pattern of the parlour rug, when suddenly I
tripped and fell against a table. The table swayed and then
righted itself, but not before a glass lamp fell over onto the
floor and broke in a thousand pieces. My father heard the
crash, and came rushing in, pen in one hand, a sheet of paper
in the other. He saw the lamp immediately, and fixed me with
his terrible look. "Who did that?" he roared. "Did you break
that lamp?"

"No!" The answer was out before I had time to think. "The
dog rushed by just now and caught the cord! And over it went!
Jason! It was Jason!" My fear had been terrible, but what I was
feeling now was a hundred times worse. I stood on the carpet

as though turned to stone, listening while he shouted for Jason
Then I held my hands over my ears while he beat the dog
hearing his squeals through my palms.

I went into my room and crawled into bed, making myself
as small as possible. I cannot describe the weight of my guilt
When Jason crept into the room, tail between his legs, I picked
him up and held him with a shame and a remorse that was
boundless, patting him, stroking him, whispering, "I'm sorry!
I'm sorry! Forgive me, Jason!" I knew I must confess, and yet
I also knew I must *not* confess, all at the same time. For if I did
tell him, my father would never forgive me that lie; if I did not,
I felt that the warm face of heaven would be hidden from me
for all time, that God would forever turn His back upon me. I
didn't cry. Sorrow was not what I was feeling. I felt a numbing
fear, and a regret so deep that I was drowning in it. Lost grace.
That's what I felt. Grace irrevocably removed from me.

I feel so ashamed of the things I have told you about my
father. I have made him sound like an ogre in a fairy tale. He
wasn't. He gave away a fifth of his small salary to the church.
He allowed himself no luxuries. He visited the sick and the
dying, and his sermons were thrilling, inspiring. Ladies in the
congregation sometimes cried while he was speaking. He
wanted everyone in the world to be good.

You maybe can't believe it, but I worried about that lamp,
that lie, for four years. I rehearsed speeches that I never
delivered; I prayed for forgiveness, but felt there could be no
forgiveness without confession. I would watch other children
playing, strangers walking briskly along the street, animals
running in the fields and think, "Oh, to be one of them,
without this binding burden on my heart." I went about my
everyday living — going to school, playing ball, drying the
dishes — but always in a small part of my heart or head was
this hard core of guilt, this feeling that I was doomed unless or
until I told my father what had really happened to that lamp.

Samantha came and talked to me today. I like her. She lacks

refinement, but she is warm and quick and passionate, which is more than you can say of either Luther or his father — both cold fish, and very virtuous and upright. And controlled. It is a terrible and unnatural thing to say about one's own son, but I do not altogether like Luther. I love him, of course. That is a different thing entirely. But his heart is squeezed and arrogant, and I often do not like him at all. Gerald is the spontaneous one, and kind.

As for me, I don't know what I am.

But I can tell you one thing. I can feel it in the air. Samantha likes me.

❖ ❖ ❖

January 11

I know I'll never be able to show you this book. I reread yesterday's entry, and was shocked to see that I had called my own son and my husband *cold fish*.

I broke the lamp when I was eight. One day when I was twelve, my father and I were looking through an old family album in the parlour. "Wait," he said. "It's getting dark. I'll get a lamp." He brought a lamp from his study, and placed it on the same table that had held the first ill-fated lamp. I heard myself speaking as though it were someone else, as though a piece of quite casual information were being offered. I had rehearsed the words so often that when they finally came out they emerged without tone or emphasis. They might have been the tapping of typewriter keys.

"Father," I heard the voice say. "Remember the old glass lamp? The one that used to be on this table?"

"Uh? Oh, yes, I guess so."

"Well, it was me that broke it."

I don't know what I expected. Probably a spectacular display of rage or an icy comment upon my sin, followed by a promise of eternal damnation. I think I had also half hoped for a thunder of drums or the sweet swell of violin strings, to accompany the end of my long period of fear and guilt.

But not much of anything happened.

"Oh?" he said. "Did you?" But I could see that he had long ago forgotten the episode. Or possibly he was too preoccupied by what he was looking at to pay much attention. Not that it mattered all that much, not really. It is true that I was relieved. But I also knew in that moment, without the smallest doubt, that crime never pays. If retribution does not come from without, it will surely always come from within. Look at what I had suffered during the past four years. I would watch my step even more carefully in future.

❖ ❖ ❖

January 12

I can see by looking at old photographs that as a teenager I was pretty. I was also shapely. I can remember mother's shy remarks to me about my clothes. "Your father wants you to stop wearing that red dress, dear. He says that it makes your bust too obvious. He says that modesty is a woman's most attractive feature." I think now that she said this a bit wistfully, being flat as a board herself. I would have felt better if he had called breasts *breasts*. Bust is a terrible word. It smacks of corseted spinsters or of plaster of Paris. When I wore the clothes I liked, I felt cheap and vulgar. When I wore the kind of things he wanted me to wear, I felt droopy, desexed, undesirable. Either way I was a loser.

But Jamie desired me. Blousy tops, loose waists and all, he still looked at me as though I were a mixture of Lana Turner, a chocolate milkshake, and a delicate flower.

❖ ❖ ❖

January 13

I am going to write about Jamie now.

Jamie worked at Sullivan's Garage after school, so he didn't have much time for parties or dating. But during the spring when I was sixteen, he spent every one of his spare moments stationed in the vacant lot across the road from our house, or walking up and down the street, kicking stones in front of him as he went. If I came out the front door, his face would burst wide open with joy, and he would come forward to accompany me wherever I was going. When Father found out that his mother had once been charged with petty theft, he told me that I must never bring him into the house and that I must never under any circumstances accept any invitations from him. But even Father could not refuse him access to the vacant lot or to the municipal sidewalk. Or so I thought.

One day, quite by accident, I saw Jamie downtown. We met eye to eye over the mittens and gloves section of Woolworth's; face aflame, he reached over and touched one of my cheeks and then kissed me most tenderly on the other. Such an innocent and lovely thing. It was my first kiss of any kind, and I came very close indeed to falling headfirst into the mittens. But Father saw us; he was standing not ten feet away, in the hardware department.

When I returned home, Father explained to me where such behaviour might lead. To the Devil, to Hell, to social disgrace, but more important, to the East Concook Home for unmarried mothers. One day when I returned alone from an errand downtown, I saw Father talking to Jamie at the end of our walk. They were both gone by the time I reached the house, so I never knew what had taken place between them. But Jamie never returned. The vacant lot remained vacant, and the sidewalk bare. I thought I would die, but I did not.

❖ ❖ ❖

January 14

I have just reread what I wrote yesterday, and it all came back to me so vividly. Not my love for Jamie, but the sweet heat and flavour of that time.

I don't think I feel like writing today.

❖ ❖ ❖

January 16

After Jamie, Father was vigilant. I was young, too young to marry. But if there had been one Jamie, there might be others. Father really did love me. He wanted me to be safe. Safe for what? For heaven, I guess. Or for my own life, although that's hardly likely. Maybe for *him*, for his love and anxiety's sake. I must try to believe that, because I'm crying less these past few days. Instead, I'm feeling angry.

Father brought Meredith home for dinner because he was new in town and probably lonely. Or so he said. More than likely, for a certainty, in fact, he had checked his credentials. Twenty-eight to my eighteen. Staunch member of the Presbyterian church and a generous contributor to the building fund. Immaculately dressed in navy suits with white shirts, blindingly white, with starched collars. Well spoken. Courteous. Six feet one inch, undeniably handsome. And with a good, dependable job.

Gerald came to me today and begged me to argue his case with his father. He is very unhappy. I went to Meredith and told him I thought Samantha was a kind and loving person, and that Gerald was after all an adult who should make his own decisions. You cannot imagine how much courage it took for me to do this. Or maybe you can, it being your business to understand this kind of thing. Meredith does not rant and rave like Father. This quality is what drew me to him in the first place. I did not then realize that anger has many faces, and that there are a lot of subtler forms of violence and violation. Meredith looked at me very coldly, and said, "I cannot imagine how anyone supposedly clever can be so stupid. You claim to love this boy, and yet you are perfectly willing to wreck his life. I forbid you to side with him. Your view of love is naive and permissive. Kindly leave this matter entirely to me." When I tried to interrupt, he broke in and said, "Allison. If you please. I do not wish to discuss this further."

I can't really see that writing all these things down is very helpful. It is true that I am crying less. But I'm not sure that it is any improvement to be feeling this terrible new anger and frustration.

I gathered up some rugs today and hung them outside on the line. Then I took a heavy stick and beat them and beat them, until the yard was a fog of dust. I did not even feel tired when I finished, and then I went inside and slept for two hours. Meredith was not pleased when supper was late, but said nothing. He sighed a great deal, however. I wanted to kick him. Or to hang him on the line and beat him with a stick.

❖ ❖ ❖

January 20

I'm remembering things that I must have shoved away to the back of my mind. I don't understand how your brain can let this happen. Surely significant things, good or bad, should be written in headlines on the forefront of one's brain. But no. Apparently not.

I have remembered something that happened the summer after my innocent fling with Jamie. I was seventeen, and I was delivering some of my mother's homemade bread to an old lady who was sick. Mrs. Bellamy was her name. She lived on the other side of town, and I took a short cut across O'Donahue's field to get there. This was not really a field, but a wild rough place with two hills, a lot of bushes, and a little creek. On my way across the smaller of the hills, I decided to go down by the creek to see if there were any Indian pipes. What I found by the edge of the water were not Indian pipes, but my father and Miss Henderson, the director of the junior choir. They were kissing. They didn't see me.

Try as I will, I can't remember one single other thing about that morning. Whether or not the bread ever reached old Mrs. Bellamy I do not know. However, I do recall hearing my mother and father talking in the kitchen that afternoon. She was speaking.

"Mr. O'Toole said he tried to get you on the church phone this morning, but that no one answered."

There was a pause. And then my father said, "Then he must have been calling the wrong number. I never left the office all morning."

I now recollect trying to argue myself out of what I had seen and heard, much as one tries to talk oneself into a belief in Santa Claus after seeing one's mother filling the stockings. Maybe that wasn't really my father down there. I brushed aside the evidence — his diamond socks (knitted by my mother) sticking out below his trouser cuffs; his briefcase on the ground beside him, with his gold initials on it (gift of the Missionary Society) — and said to myself, *It was not him, it was not him.* And if it had not been my father, then I had not heard him tell that lie. Then I forgot about it for twenty-eight years.

Meredith has told Gerald that if he marries Samantha he must leave the company, Meredith Wentworth and Sons Limited. Gerald came and asked my opinion and advice. He said he had always hated working for the company anyway, but had done it because of "family pressure." Family pressure, my foot, I thought. Let us call a spade a spade, if you please. Father pressure. I knew that Gerald had once wanted to be a garage mechanic; as Jamie had been exactly that, I guess I had not looked on it as such a disgraceful thing to be. But Meredith had refused to consider it for two seconds. Pride. The First Deadly Sin.

I told Gerald that I had been forbidden to offer advice or to discuss this matter with him.

"Please, Mom," he begged. "*Please*. I probably know what I'm going to do anyway, but tell me what you think, how you feel about it."

"Do you love her a great deal?" I asked.

"Yes," he said. "Oh, yes."

"Then leave," I said. "The company will survive. And so will we. And so will you." Then I kissed him.

I am feeling neither angry nor weepy tonight. I am feeling rather pleased with myself.

❖ ❖ ❖

February 1

What a month this has been. I may become a chronic diarist. I won't pretend that it solves everything. I'm feeling like a cracked egg — very, very fragile. But *ready*. Do you know what I mean?

When Meredith heard from Gerald that he was leaving the company, he came to me and cried. *Cried!* If you had asked me, I would have said that all Meredith's tears had dried up at birth, that there was no room in this man for fury or grief or for passionate responses. So life is full of surprises. I comforted him. I felt like the strong one.

And that night I was visited by another memory.

When I was eighteen years old — several months before I met Meredith — I was struck by a car. I was not hurt, but I was taken to the hospital for routine examination. Insurance regulations required it. Word reached my parents that there had been an accident, before they received the news that I had not been injured. When they arrived at the hospital, Father pushed my mother aside and rushed to where I sat on a straight chair in the emergency ward. He took me in his arms and held me so tightly that I remember hurting all over. "Thank God, thank God you're safe!" he gasped. "Oh, Allison, I'm so sorry, so sorry! Forgive me. Try to forgive me. Oh, my child, thank God you are safe!" Then he put his head down on my shoulder and cried like a child. Much of that scene is fuzzy in my memory. And I don't know what any of it means, or why I forgot it. But whatever else he may have meant, I can see now that two messages were clear. One, he was a human being after all. Two, he loved me very much. In any case, my moment of truth was short-lived, because I fainted soon afterwards. When I came to, the scene was locked away where it was very hard to find.

❖ ❖ ❖

February 15

Samantha and Gerald are to be married on April 2nd. Meredith has told Gerald that he may remain in the company after all, but Gerald has informed him (very nicely) that (thank you very much) he's already been accepted for a course in automechanics at the community college. He has some money saved. Besides, Samantha has a job. Meredith took this hard, but he is trying to adjust to all the new things that are happening to him. Luther is not trying to adjust to anything at all, although yesterday I astonished him by telling him he was an insufferable snob. I hope he will think about that. If this makes him angry with me, that's just too bad. Jane can prop him up, and I'm sure she will.

Samantha's mother died when she was ten, so I am helping her with her wedding dress. She has a flair for design, and I am good with a needle. The pattern is a bit extreme, but she has the looks and the figure to carry it off. We will keep it our secret until the wedding day. She is warm and communicative, and I think she is going to be the daughter I have always longed for. She says she has a lot to learn from me. She doesn't realize how much I need to learn from her.

Meredith will be all right. He hasn't really changed. It's just that now I'm ready to see things in him that must have been there all along. If you lie right down on your belly, yes, I said *belly*, with your face pressed flat into the floor, you can't criticize people if they walk over you. My mother was a doormat all her life, and I can't say I look back on her with any feeling stronger than a tender pity. I know it irritated Meredith when I was going through that weepy phase, and I can't say I blame him. Yesterday he said something arrogant to me, and I said to him, "Meredith, you are not God Almighty, and I would appreciate a little humility around here." He was obviously dumbfounded; but it was also clear that he preferred this approach to that of the teary-eyed wimp. He is not my idea of Lochinvar riding out of the west, and never was. But we'll manage. We'll be fine.

I never had any intention of showing you this diary. Not really. But maybe I will. I'm even tempted to invite you to the wedding. I feel that you are sort of responsible for it. One way or another.

MR. MANUEL JENKINS

I REMEMBER WELL THE DAY he came. It was autumn, which starts early in Nova Scotia, and is always for me a time of joy and bitterness. The summer is so short and the fall so brilliantly beautiful that it is like watching the final illness of a loved one, who suddenly takes on a special loveliness as death approaches. And in some parts of the province, winter can seem as forever as dying. As early as the second week in August, my mother would say, "I feel fall in the air," and my heart would lurch a little.

It was late September, and some of the low-lying bushes were already scarlet against the black of the evergreen forest. Dried flowers waved stiffly against the blue of the bay, but the gulls were acting as though nothing had changed, as though sailing above on the wind currents were enough for them, now and for always.

It had been a bad day for me, and the splendour of the afternoon rebuked me. Beauty can be an aching thing when you are unhappy, and I have always welcomed fog and rain — or better still, a storm — when I am sad. Otherwise, I can feel a pull back to balance; and misery, for me, has always been half in love with itself.

The reasons for my depression were not dramatic. No one had died; the house had not burned down; I hadn't failed a test in school or lost a boyfriend. But I was fifteen, a time of limbo for me, and a period of trigger-happy nerves. Neither child nor woman, I wanted to be both and sometimes neither. For one thing, I longed to adore my mother again; but she irritated me almost beyond endurance, with her obsession with food and cleanliness and good behaviour — and with her refusal to listen to what I was or was not saying. I wanted her to see right into my head and heart and to congratulate me on their contents. Instead, she ignored or misconstrued or *misdirected* even the things I said aloud. For instance, that morning I had said to her, "Mom, it's such a divine day. I'm going to take the boat out to Crab Island and just sit on a rock and be me all day long."

To which she replied, "You can be you right here in the kitchen this very minute and help me defrost the fridge." Which I did. After that she said, "What's the use of going out to Crab Island all by yourself? You could at least take Sarah with you. She's been galumphing around the house and driving me crazy. If you go alone, she won't even have the boat to play in." And where did that leave me? Either I stayed home and nursed the hot ball of resentment that inhabited my stomach almost constantly of late; or I went to the island with Sarah, age twelve, whose main characteristic was never shutting up for one second, and who always wanted to be *doing* something — like *exploring*, or *skipping stones*, or writing X's and O's on the granite cliff with rocks — *scrape, scrape, scrape* — when I'd be wanting to soak up the stillness. I opted for home and the hot ball of resentment.

My mom was the big boss in our home. Do this, do that, and we all did it. Jump! and we jumped. Even my dad jumped. He had a slow and kindly heart, unending patience, and a warm smile. That had been enough for me for years and years. But suddenly this year it wasn't. I wanted him to look my mother in the eye and say, "I live here, too. I caught that fish you're frying in the pan. If I want to go hunting this afternoon, I'll go. And you can just stop ordering me around like I was in kindergarten." But that morning he'd spoken to her as she was thunking down the rolling pin on the cookie dough at the kitchen table. "Gert," he said slowly, tentatively, as though he already anticipated her answer, "I thought maybe I'd go over to Barrington this afternoon and see old Sam Hiltz. Haven't had a visit with him for near two years. I'm kind of tuckered out. Feel like I could sort of use a day off."

"We could all use a day off," she said tartly, no softness in her anywhere. "If women ever took a day off, their families would starve to death in twenty-four hours. And by the time they got back, they'd have to spend longer than their day off cleaning up the bathroom and the kitchen." She delivered to him a piercing look. "Why, I can go shopping in Shelburne for two hours, and come back to find the kitchen sink looking like the washbasin at the drive-in." She stopped attacking the dough and started forming shapes with the cookie-cutter. No diamonds or hearts on that pan, ever. Or chickens or ginger-bread men. All her cookies were round. "And do you think these cookies drop out of the sky?" she went on. "Chocolate chips all firmly in place? Or that an angel flies down and deposits your clean laundry on the bed each Monday evening? No siree. I need that car this afternoon to pick up a parcel at Sears. Old Sam can wait till the next time you feel a holiday coming over you. And if you've got that little to do, how about bringing in some water. Or wood. Or lettuce from the garden. Or *something*."

I wanted to take the pans of round cookies, all the same size, all placed exactly one-half inch from each other, and throw them through the window. I imagined the crash as they hit the window, visualized the little slivers of glass protruding from the dough. And I wanted to yell at my sweet and silent father, *Do* something! *Answer* her! Say, It's my car. I paid for it. Go to Sears *tomorrow*. Old Sam is ninety-two years old and sick, and he might die this afternoon.

Or he could have said, To hell with all that food! Curses on your stupid cookies! We're all overweight in this family, all six of us. And we don't need to be that *clean*. Even without any plumbing, some people live to be a hundred and ten years old. Sit down. Fold your hands. Take the time to talk to us a spell. Or better still, to listen.

But no. Off he went, down to the government wharf to discuss the day's catch with his friends.

And outside the kitchen, the soft gold September sun shed radiance upon the face of the sea. The sky was cloudless, and almost as blue as the bay. Such beauty was beckoning, and not one of us could see.

And then he came. Straight up to the front door, where no one ever came. Knocking three times, he waited, hat in hand, and I opened the door.

The loveliness of the day had left me, but there was no way to escape the beauty of the stranger who stood before me. He was tanned and shining, face strong and gentle, body tall, hard, powerful.

"Got a room?" he said, rolling a toothpick around in his mouth.

"Pardon?" I asked. My mother's zeal for food and cleanliness stretched itself to include language. She never let anyone forget that she had once been a schoolteacher.

"Got a room? I bin lookin' all over. I'm workin' on th' new road, and need a boardin' place."

I hardly heard what he said, I was that busy looking. Even the toothpick wove a spell for me, probably because of the way his lips moved around it.

"Well?" He grinned. "Cat got yer tongue?"

"Just a minute," I said, and went to deliver his message to my mother.

"Certainly not!" she snapped, wiping the flour off her hands with a damp cloth. "As if I didn't have enough to do as it is."

I wanted to get down on my knees and plead. Please, Mother. I'll do anything, if you'll just keep him. I'll come home from school and cook his meals. I'll do his laundry. Only please,

Mom. Can't we let him stay, for a little while anyway, just so I can *look* at him?

She came to the door, still wiping her hands. The toothpick was missing, and the beautiful stranger stood before her, quiet, still. I watched her, hope waning. But a flicker remained. I knew that we needed money. I also knew that my brother's room was empty. I stayed close to her, as though hoping that some of my eagerness would seep into her.

Even in her apron, with the white kerchief tied around her hair, my mother was a pretty woman. At forty, she still had a young face and firm skin. She was tanned from hours of blueberry picking and from weeding the garden, and the only flaw in her face was a line between her brows — a mark of worry or of irritation, which came and went. She reached the door, the line intact. And then her face changed. I cannot say how it changed. The line was still there, and she was not smiling. But for a few moments, there was something about her that was unfamiliar to me.

Then she said, with more courtesy than I would have expected, "I'm sorry, but I have four children at home, and too much work to do already. You could try Mrs. Schultz across the way."

"I tried Mrs. Schultz," he said. "I tried everyone. I bin everywhere. I even bin to Mr. Snow and asked him if I could sleep in th' barn. Please, ma'am," — he smiled — "I wouldn't be no bother. I could cook my own meals. Just a room would be fine."

"Well . . . " she said slowly, as though to herself, "there's Jeffery's room empty, now that he's away in Upper Canada . . ." Then she was silent for a moment or two, staring across the bay, with that line deep between her eyebrows.

"Yes," she said suddenly, but sighing. "I guess we could manage. But you'll eat with us." No way she'd be letting any stranger go messing around in her kitchen. "Will you be needing the room for long, Mr. . . . ?" she inquired.

"No, ma'am," he answered. "Two months maybe. Could be three. Nothin' you can do, once the frost hits hard. Manuel. Manuel Jenkins. I'm much obliged."

He picked up his suitcase and walked in, filling the kitchen with his beauty, blessing the walls, casting light and gladness upon stove, table, electric clock. Like one of the wheeling gulls, I flew out into the back field and up, up to the top of the hill, running all the way. There I threw myself down among the high grasses and the late goldenrod, face turned to the sky. Nothing mattered. Nothing. My mother could crab and fuss and complain all she wanted. My dad could roll over like the Jacksons' yellow dog and wait to be kicked, for all I cared. The beautiful stranger had come, and would live in my brother's room for two months. I would hear him moving about next door to me, doing his mysterious ablutions. Through the vent I could maybe hear him breathing. He would be there at suppertime, casting a benediction upon us by his presence, with his smile, his dark skin, his enormous hands with their oddly graceful fingers. I turned over and pressed my face into the grass, blinded by so bright a vision.

❖ ❖ ❖

Our first meal with Manuel Jenkins was an event to remember. My mother sat at one end of the table, straight as a stick, company manners written all over her face. My father sat at the other end, comfortable, relaxed, slumped in his chair, waiting for the mashed turnips to reach him. When they did, he lit into his food as though, if he didn't attack it immediately, it would vanish from the plate. My mother often reprimanded him about this. "I've spent a long hour and a half preparing this meal," she'd say. "There's no law that says it has to disappear in nothing flat." Or "This is a dining room, Harvey Nickerson, not a barn." To which he paid not the slightest heed whatsoever. It seemed to be the one area where she couldn't move him. Tonight I looked at him and thought, C'mon, Dad.

Just for the next couple of months, let's eat slowly, like fancy people. Mr. Jenkins is here. What will he think if we eat like savages?

What indeed? I looked across the table at Mr. Jenkins, and watched him stuff his napkin in the neck of his T-shirt, revealing a veritable carpet of black hairs upon his chest. Then he ate. Holding the fork in his fist like a trowel, he shovelled Mom's enormous meal into himself in perhaps five minutes. And noisily, with quite a lot of smacking and chomping. And, when drinking his hot tea, slurping. I didn't mind. He could have eaten his entire meal with his bare hands, and it would have been all the same to me. But I dared not look at my mother. She would never allow anyone to live in our house with table manners like that. Then out came the toothpick, and I watched entranced as it wandered around his mouth without the aid of his fingers. It was as though it had a life of its own. Then he wiped his mouth with the back of his hand, pulled one of Polly's pigtails, smiled his dazzling smile, scraped his chair back, and said, "Much obliged, ma'am. That was some good." And was gone.

I looked at my mother. What would she say, feel, do? Mr. Jenkins had just spent the mealtime doing everything we had always been forbidden to do. Would she make him leave? Would she hate him? But she was just sitting there, arms and hands slack, staring at the tablecloth, registering nothing. After all, she had said he could stay. If she kept her word, she was stuck with him. The kids, who had spent half an hour with him before dinner, were all aglow, loving his cheerfulness, his handsome face, his bigness, his booming laugh.

Then he was back.

"S'cuse me, ma'am," he said, "I'm forgettin' m' manners. This here's a lot o' people and a lot o' food. Like you said this morning, you're a hard-workin' lady. You must be some tired." Then he picked up his dishes from the table, washed them in the kitchen sink, and placed then with amazing delicacy in the dish drainer to dry. "Why, thank you, Mr. Jenkins," said Mom, her face expressionless, although for a moment the line disappeared from between her eyebrows. But I remembered his dirty fingernails, and I wondered how she felt about having them in her clean dishwater. Later I saw her change the water before she washed the other dishes.

"Seems like a nice enough man," said my father, as he stuffed his pipe full of tobacco. Then he pushed away the dishes on the table, to make room for a game of crib with Julien.

❖ ❖ ❖

We were given three and one-half months with Mr. Jenkins. The frost kept off, and the early winter was as mild as April. We had him with us until January 6th. Three months, fifteen days, and six hours.

Except for my father, we all called him Mr. Jenkins. He was, my mother surmised, about thirty-eight years old, and therefore we were to treat him with the respect befitting an older man — although we all called Aggie Crowell's grandmother Susie, and old Sam was always Sam to us kids. I tried to keep my face inscrutable, but maybe Mom saw the glint in my eye and wanted to place distance between me and him. In any case, I used to call him Manuel privately, when I was alone in my room. "Manuel, Manuel," I would whisper, rolling the name around my tongue, loving the sound, the taste of it.

But it didn't really matter what she made us call him. Calling a man mister couldn't change the way the rest of us felt about him. Even my dad. I think even he was half in love with that towering stranger, in a way that had nothing to do with sex. He grew to love him the way you love a rocky cliff, or a heron in flight, or a sunfish turning its giant body on the surface of the sea. Or a clown dancing on the street in the midday sun.

Most of us, of course, didn't see him too often. All the kids except Polly were in school, and that just left weekends and suppertime and a small slice of evening, before he'd go up to his room and read his *Popular Mechanics* magazines and listen to his radio. And my dad was always off fishing by 6:00 A.M., gone all day. Mr. Jenkins got his lunch at our place, but no one was there except my mother and Polly and the dog, unless it was on weekends.

Weekends were heaven for me. He didn't have much to do with me directly. But I watched as he made our home a sunshiny place, filling our little house with his huge and animal grace, his laughter, his easy way with life and living. He's like an enormous cat, I thought, a panther, maybe. Working when necessary, but knowing how to relax, how to play, how to soak up the sun, letting his cubs crawl all over him as he radiates serenity. Our kids all followed him around like the Pied Piper, and he never seemed to mind. Polly was four, and he'd sit with her on his lap and talk to her as though she were twenty-five years of age. "How was your day, Polly girl?" he'd ask, and then he'd really listen when she told him about her dolls and the dog and the drawings she had made. I wondered about her sitting on his dirty overalls in her clean dresses, but my mother made no comment. Politeness to guests was almost as high on her list as cleanliness.

Julien had Mr. Jenkins up on a pedestal so high that it's a wonder he didn't fall off. The two of them would go out before supper and play catch, and once Mr. Jenkins took him to show him the front-end loader he worked on. He let Julien sit way up on top in the driver's seat, and waited around for a whole half hour while Julien pretended he was driving it. When Julien came home, his eyes were like pie plates.

Even Sarah. Gabby old Sarah who never shut up. He'd sit on the old swing with her, chewing a blade of grass, while she'd talk on and on and on. And he'd smile and nod, saying things like "That so?" or "Well, *well*," or "I bet you enjoyed *that*!" Never once did he fall asleep in the middle of all that talk, which is what all the rest of us always wanted to do. And Mr. Jenkins was a man who could fall asleep on the head of a pin in the middle of a thunderstorm, if he wanted to.

Happy though I was, I never got over the small niggling fear that Mom would finally make him leave, because of all the bad things he did. He left his shoes around where you could trip over them, although I tried to protect him — and us — by putting them by the doorway every time I found them in the wrong place. He chewed gum with his mouth open, and passed some around for all of us to do the same. My mother would chew hers with her small mouth tightly shut, slowly, as though it tasted either very good or very bad — I could never be sure which. And his belongings — his magazines, his clothes, his tools — littered the house, or decorated it, depending on your point of view — from top to bottom and side to side. My mom, I thought, must have needed that board money really badly.

One evening, early on, during maybe the third week of his stay, my father came home extra tired from lobstering. It had been a day of driving rain, and he was chilled to the bone and grey with fatigue. Everyone was supposed to take off shoes and boots at the door, and he always did; but on that day he sort of moved like a person in a trance, right into the middle of the kitchen floor. My mother flew at him and pushed him backwards to the doorway, her voice hard, as if it were hammering on something metal.

"Inconsiderate! Always inconsiderate! Not one thought for the length of time it takes to scrub a floor! You get out into the back porch and take those wet clothes off before the kitchen looks like a slum. And hurry. Dinner's ready. You're late! I'm not going to wait two more seconds." My dad just stood there for a moment, as though he had been struck physically, and then he turned toward the porch.

Then Mr. Jenkins spoke.

"Jest a sweet minute, ma'am," he said, his voice soft and coaxing. "We all knows you works hard. We're all right grateful to you for your good food and all that scrubbin' and polishin'. But anyone can see with half an eye that that man o' yours is three-quarters dead with bein' tired." He said all this in a lazy quiet way, but his eyes, always so kind and warm, were steely cold and serious as death.

"Now, Sarah girl," he went on, "you jest get up and wash them few dirty spots off your mom's floor. Won't take but a minute. And Julien — I think your dad could use your help. Maybe you could put his wet boots out behind the stove to dry them out a bit. And you, m'girl," he said, turning to me, "how about a bottle o' beer for your dad, before he falls right over dead." He said all this from the couch by the back window. He never moved a muscle. Just sort of organized the whole lot of us into a rescue brigade. I thought that would be the end of Mr. Jenkins. I'd never my whole life long heard anyone tell my mother to shut up, and that's really what he was doing. But she just turned quickly back to the stove and started shoving pots around, this way and that. When we all finally sat down to supper, there wasn't any tension left at all — not in me, anyway. Mr. Jenkins sat up, talking with his mouth full, and told us about life up in the James Bay territory, when he was working on the new highway up there. His huge brown body, sandwiched between Julien and Polly, was like one of the statues I'd seen in our ancient history book. I was sick with longing for him, but also oddly content just to sit peacefully at a distance and feast my eyes upon his grace of body and person. For me, the slurp of his tea was like background music. I always avoided my mother's eyes at the dinner table. As time went by, I knew she would not evict him, but I felt I could not bear it if she scolded him, like us, for his table manners.

When Christmastime came, Mr. Jenkins said he was leaving for the four-day holiday. The kids all kicked up a terrible row, and my dad begged him to stay. "Surely they can do without you at home just this one year," he said.

"Well," said Mr. Jenkins, grinning sheepishly, "truth to tell, home is where I hangs my hat at any given time. If you wants me to stay, that I will do, thanking you most kindly." Then he excused himself and took the bus to Yarmouth, and was gone for ten hours.

On Christmas Day, we found out what he had done with those ten hours. He had gone shopping. And shopping and shopping. He bought extra lights for the tree and a wreath for the door. He supplied a bottle of real champagne and another of sparkling wine that I was allowed to taste, and there was pink lemonade for the kids. He had even bought tall glasses with stems — seven of them — for all of us. He gave Polly a doll that said six different things when you pulled a string in her back. For Julien he had an exact model of his front-end loader, and I thought Julien might possibly faint for joy. Sarah got three Nancy Drew books, and for me he bought a silver bracelet with "Sterling" written inside it. He gave my dad a big red wool sweater to keep him warm in the lobster boat, no matter how cold it got. To my mother, he presented a gold chain with a small amethyst pendant. We all had gifts for him, too, either bought or made or cooked, and the day was one of the single most perfect days I have ever known.

If Christmas was a perfect day, the day that came two weeks later was a terrible one. We all knew he had to leave soon, that the deep frost would not stay away forever. But when he actually stood there in the kitchen, holding his suitcase, it seemed that all that was warm and beautiful in our lives was about to abandon us. I could not imagine the supper table without him, the couch empty, the silence that would strike me from Jeffrey's room. He shook hands with my dad and my mother. My dad pumped his hand and said, "Come again, Manuel, and good luck." My mother stood erect as ever, and said, "It was a pleasure to have you here, Mr. Jenkins," and almost sounded as though she meant it. Polly and Sarah cried, and he hugged them both. Then he tossed Julien up in the air and shook his hand. Julien didn't say a single word, because it took his whole strength just to keep from crying. Then Mr. Jenkins came and shook my hand and kissed me lightly on the top of my head. "Have a good life, m'girl," he said, and smiled such a smile at me, oh such a smile. Then he walked to the door.

A lot is said about the value of strong, silent men. Me, I think that men who are silent about things that matter just don't have the strength to say what they really feel. Manuel Jenkins turned around at the doorway and said, "Thank you. I'll be missing you a whole lot. I loves you all." Then he was gone. I put on my warm jacket and boots and went back to the old sawmill and sat inside on a bench. Over by the breakwater, the gulls were screaming, screaming, and I could hear the winter wind rattling the broken windows. I had taken several of my dad's big handkerchiefs with me, because I knew I was going to be doing a lot of crying.

The whole family just sort of limped through the next few weeks, but gradually we emerged from our grief and got on with our lives. My mother would say things like "My word, he was only a man. Perk up, Julien. It isn't the end of the world." Or to Polly and Sarah, "For goodness' sake, stop sighing. At least we're not falling all over his shoes, and there's a lot less work for me to do." And to my dad, "Don't look so sad, Harvey. He's not the only one on earth who can play crib. C'mon. I'll have a game with you." One day she said to me, not unkindly, right out of the blue, "He was too old for you. You'll find your own man sometime, and he'll be right for you. Let Mr. Jenkins go." I wasn't even mad. I didn't know why.

One day in early February, I was sent home from school with a high fever. The vice-principal drove me to the front gate. I entered the house by the back door and took off my boots in the porch. Then, slowly, because I was not feeling well, I dragged myself upstairs. At the top of the stairs I stopped short, unable to go forward or back. There, to the right of me, beyond her doorway, was my mother, sitting in front of her dressing table. Her forehead was right down on the table top and was lying on her left hand. The other hand was stretched out across the top, and was in a tight fist. I was very frightened. I had never before seen my mother in any state of weakness whatsoever. She seemed never to be sick, and I had never heard her give voice to any physical pain. She was always strong, sure, in perfect control. A heart attack, I thought, and dared not speak lest I alarm her. Then, as I waited, a long terrible sigh shook her, and she opened her closed fist. Then she closed it and sighed again. In her hand was the gold chain and the amethyst pendant.

I crept down the stairs in my stocking feet, and put on my outdoor clothes in the back porch. Then I retraced my steps to the front gate, fever and all, and slammed it shut. Returning to the back porch, I stomped the snow off my feet on the stoop, and entered the house, banging the door behind me. I was long and slow taking my clothes off, and by the time I was hanging up my scarf, my mother appeared in the kitchen.

"What's wrong?" she said, her voice warm and concerned. "Why are you home so early?" I realized for the first time that she had become gentler, and that she had been like that for a long time. Even to my father. Possibly especially to my father. As I mounted the stairs to bed, I pondered these things; but none of them made much sense to me.

You maybe thought I was telling you this tale about Mr. Manuel Jenkins because there was something secret and terrible in his past that we eventually found out about. But no. Or possibly you were looking for something dramatic at the end, like the Mounties coming to get him, or a tragic death under the front-end loader. But none of these things happened. He just came. And then he just went. None of us, not one of us, ever saw him again. He never wrote to us, which seemed odd to me at the time, because he was a great one for saying thank-you. So I think now that perhaps he didn't know how to write. Maybe those big hands of his never held a pencil. Come to think of it, he never would join the kids when they did their crossword puzzles. "Too hard for me," he'd say, chuckling, and we always thought he was joking. No. He just left. Disappeared down the road in his front-end loader, and was swallowed up by the hill behind Mrs. Fitzgerald's house.

I'm forty-one years old now, and from time to time I still ache to see Manuel Jenkins. I'm happily married to a husband whom I love most dearly, and I have four beautiful children. But I feel as though something is unfinished. Does that seem curious to you? It's like seeing a really great movie and having to leave the theatre ten minutes before the end. Or like wanting a teddy bear all your whole life long, and not ever having one. Or like yearning to see, just once more, the rocky coast where you grew up. And I'm exactly the age my mother was when he left. Sometimes I think that if I could see him just once more, I might understand everything, all of it. And that then I could put the memory of him away where it belongs. Although I live on a farm in the middle of Saskatchewan, I have a notion that one of these days I'll just turn around, and there he'll be at the back door, filling the kitchen with his size and with his grace.

It could happen, you know. I feel it could.

❖

LYSANDRA'S
POEM

WHEN I WAS A CHILD, my family lived beside the sea. But not precisely so. Not right on the edge of the Atlantic Ocean, with the horizon sliding away flat all the way to Spain. No. We lived in a little harbour town in Nova Scotia, a full mile from any point of land where you could view the open sea. But apart from the fact that you couldn't see the ocean (except insofar as the harbour was a part of it), the sea might just as well have been smack dab in the middle of our town. A day without fog was a time for rejoicing. Most days, tourists crept through our streets in their shiny American cars, fresh off the Bar Harbour ferry from sunny New England, headlights on and honking. The winters were windy and damp and dispiriting, the springs endless and fluky — promising summer one day and sprinkling snow on the stunted tulips the next. In summertime, all expeditions were planned tentatively; sentences ended with the phrase "if it doesn't rain." Packed linens were attacked by mildew; wire coathangers rusted; envelopes stuck together if they weren't stored in airtight plastic bags.

The fact is that we can't cope with too much fine weather in Nova Scotia. We're chicken-hearted about the heat, and are beaten down by it, ploughed right under. And a brisk sunny day — a perfect day — undoes us. People with indoor jobs are irritable, tense; spirit and body are in active resistance to any activity that takes place inside a building. Those who are free to go outside — housewives, the unemployed, mothers trailing children, people on vacation — spill out of their houses onto the water, the beaches, the parks, or their own backyards. On such a day, not all those smiling people strolling along our Main Streets are tourists. Most of them are native Nova Scotians, agape at a miracle. People call in sick, sleep through the alarm, quit jobs. If there are six or seven of these days in a row, the whole economy is at peril: editors miss deadlines; back orders are ignored; laundry accumulates; cupboards are bare. The sighting of a fog bank or the first rainy day is almost a relief.

One way or another, a climate like this is bound to rub off on people. One person may become surly and fixed, grey and dank of spirit, long-lived and persistent and a trial to his family. Another can end up hopeful — the fruit of those spectacular sunny days when the light is clearer, more pungent than most other Canadians could ever imagine; if one dwells on and in those days, an optimist is bred, living for and believing in the arrival of such rare and golden times. Or you can be the way I was, stubborn and opportunistic, snatching what I could out of a resistant environment. Or like Lysandra Cochrane, at first tentative and careful, and then with no softness in her, bitter and barbed, with a heart as hard and as cutting as diamonds.

Lysandra! you may exclaim. What a name to issue forth from such a small and simple town in one of the back places of our land. No town is simple, let me say, but that does not explain Lysandra's name. Nova Scotians — especially those in coastal areas — have a way of leafing through literature (by which I mean anything from old school texts to the Bible and the obituary columns) to find names for their babies. The Cochranes fished around in heaven knows what sources, and pulled up Lysandra. Rumour had it that Mr. Cochrane — addicted to libraries, in any case — spent the day his wife was in labour in the reference library in Halifax, looking for names. He was a smart man, a sky-high scholarship student in his day. His Dalhousie bursary had covered tuition only, and he had lacked sufficient cash to puff out the sum enough to accept it. He was one of those ones who are "grey and dank of spirit." His ambition had been snuffed out before it had had a chance to warm up, and he lived his whole adult life as a minor clerk in a law office, watching other people cash in on the benefits of a university education. He drank a large percentage of his earnings, snapped at his pale wife (once a beauty according to my mother, but my imagination failed to grasp such an improbability), and sired four thin children.

Lysandra was my best friend. She was as dark as her mother was fair, a skinny kid, all angles and elbows and bony knees. Her skin was smooth and sallow, her hair long and limp. She was tall for her age when we were kids, and shy. She looked at strangers — and at teachers and fathers — out of enormous black eyes, head bent forward and down. She walked with an awkward jerky gait, as though she were not at home on her own legs, and as she passed by, the other kids would whisper, "Pigeon-Toed Cochrane!"

But when we were alone together, Lysandra was full of amazing thoughts, large ambitions, bizarre projects. Without being instructed, she thought in metaphors, and her speech was full of exotic images and odd rhythms. She invented a whole mini-language so that she and I could talk to one another without being understood by others. She intended to be a writer — an *author*, she said — famous and rich, and this thought permeated most of her other plans and inventions. Like her father, she haunted the library, but equipped with a hope he had long ago relinquished. She read all the good poets before she was twelve, and a lot of the bad ones, too. She was gobbling up Shakespeare while I was stretched out on the floor on my stomach with *Crime Comics*. It was to her books that she retreated when her father went on his rampages, escaping his noise and the sight of her frowsy mother's stricken face — losing herself in whatever volume she had in her room, finding her place at a neatly inserted bookmark. If I were in the house at the time, we would race upstairs at the first hint of conflict, and I would watch this withdrawal. She wouldn't say a word to me, but would just sit up straight on a little yellow chair she had, her book held close to her face, not moving except to turn the pages. I both hated and relished these occasions. We didn't have high drama like this in my house, and I listened, breath held, to Mr. Cochrane's fierce catalogue of oaths — words to make me shudder all the while I was straining to keep from missing any of them. I was single-mindedly troubled by the sounds that came from Mrs. Cochrane, but this was part of the performance and had to be endured if I were to benefit from the rest of it. Besides, there was no escape for me. I could hardly march downstairs and walk through that battlefield and out the back door. I sat on the bed hunched under an afghan while Lysandra read on, her lips in a thin, tight smile.

❖ ❖ ❖

In March of the year when we were in grade 7, the principal announced a poetry contest. He told us about it during Monday morning assembly, just before the national anthem. The entries to the contest would be due on May 27th. There would be three judges, headed by Miss Alexander, the vice-principal. The other two would be Mr. Knickle, the town mayor, and Mr. Reuben, the editor of the local newspaper, the *South Shore Standard*. Thus were prestige, professionalism, and masculinity added to the team of judges.

I was standing beside Lysandra in assembly when the competition was announced. Her bent head shot up, and she stared into space with eyes so wide open that they almost frightened me. Then she looked at me with oh such a gaze of wonder, such a look of peace and triumph. When she walked out of the auditorium, her step was smooth and sure, her shoulders high. No one whispered "Pigeon-Toed Cochrane" as she passed. No one would have considered mocking such a display of calm self-confidence.

Not everyone entered the poetry contest, but our English teachers urged us to write something for it, and many of us did. However, Lysandra was the only one to devote her entire life to it, filling a whole shoe box with poetry, long before May 27th. You could see her scribbling in her loose-leaf at recess time on the school swing set, or high on the jungle gym after the little kids had gone home from school in the afternoon. On Saturdays she would do her writing out on the granite bluff overlooking the harbour, or seated at the lunch counter at the Seaway Restaurant, making her Coke last for an hour and forty-five minutes. I played with other kids during this period, because Lysandra was of no use at all to me.

The poem I entered in the contest was about a shipwreck, and it had eighteen stanzas. The rhythm went jig-a jig-a jig-a jig, and there was rhyme at the ends of lines 1 and 2 and again at 3 and 4. Like slope, dope; eat, feet. It wasn't a forced kind of rhythm or anything. The beat went along easefully without any little words tacked on to make the right number of feet. I wrote it in March, during the week after the contest was announced, so that I would have the ordeal over and done with. It was a little like getting your Christmas shopping done all in one day on the first of November.

That spring was one that most Nova Scotians will always remember. The snows melted by the end of March, and April came sailing in with sunshine and a kind of sheltering softness that was foreign to all of us. We were playing softball and kick-the-can one month ahead of time, and by mid-May people were ignoring all warnings and planting their gardens in the warm moist earth. Even Mr. Cochrane looked cheerful as he walked to and from the law office, and Lysandra floated around town, notebook held close to her chest, looking as though she were in touch with a vision; and I suppose she was. On one of the rare occasions when she had time for me, she told me that her poem was already twenty-two pages long. I asked what it was about, and she said, "Life."

"Oh." I replied. She wouldn't let me read it, but one after-noon I looked at the manuscript upside down when she spread the pages out on the bed so that I might admire its magnitude. The poetry wandered all over the sheets, with short lines and long ones, sometimes with whole sections dribbling down the centre of the page. After this unsatisfactory demonstration, she took the papers, folded them tenderly, and put them carefully back into the shoe box, stroking the top page with the flat of her hand. She closed her eyes and lifted her head as though in prayer. "I'll die if the house burns down," she said, her teeth clenched. At first I didn't understand, but then I did. I remember thinking, I hope I never love or want anything that hard. Just thinking about it exhausted me.

"You should make a copy," I said.

"Oh, well," she sighed.

❖   ❖   ❖

Of course I was a shoo-in to win that contest. Miss Alexander, the vice-principal, was about 200 years old, and had no truck with any kind of verse that didn't rhyme and wasn't of the jig-a jig-a jig variety. I had often heard her speak scathingly of "free verse": "the lazy poet's way of avoiding a lot of hard work," she'd say, lips pulled down at the corners, eyebrows drawn together behind her thick glasses. What's more, her father had been a fisherman on the Banks, and had been shipwrecked way back in 1920, when she'd been old enough to take in all the details. Those same details she liked to dole out to anyone who presented a willing ear. I liberally stacked my poem with material that was not so much lifted from her as it was spiced with the flavour of her own tale.

But there were two men on the jury. Could they not have taken Miss Alexander's prejudices and swung them around? No, they could not. Mayors do not by definition necessarily know a great deal about poetry. Mr. Knickle knew next to nothing. The principal had put him on the jury to give it status.

Mr. Knickle had agreed to serve because of political visibility. He had no intention of rocking any boats, poetic or otherwise.

Mr. Reuben, the editor of the *South Shore Standard*, knew a lot about local politics and the economic problems of the Atlantic seaboard; from time to time he wrote flat-footed editorials about these matters. He was familiar with the inequalities of freight rates and the need for federal subsidies. Poetry was not his territory. Moreover, both Mr. Knickle and Mr. Reuben had been taught by Miss Alexander when they were in grade 4. Mr. Reuben remembered what she had done when he had cracked his knuckles once too often during Silent Prayer. During the meetings of the poetry jury, Mr. Knickle had to stifle an impulse to raise his hand every time he wanted to speak.

Besides, consider my poem. Where could you find a subject better designed to please two men? A shipwreck. Men doing traditionally male things — heroic and beset by danger. I won by acclamation.

On the afternoon when the contest results were announced, we were handed back our poems. I received a wristwatch and a return ticket to Halifax; best of all, the eighteen verses of my poem were to be published in the next week's issue of the *South Shore Standard* — heady matters for a thirteen-year-old. I wound my watch noisily and put it on, arranging my face into an expression of humility.

Lysandra ran out of the schoolyard ahead of me, tripping over a discarded hockey stick and almost falling. The many pages of her poem went flying, and she had to chase around after them, rescuing them from the wind. Her face was ashen and without expression of any kind. She walked home alone, chin up, legs unsteady once again. A disembodied voice from somewhere behind me called out, "Pigeon-Toed Cochrane!"

That evening Mr. Cochrane took Lysandra's shoe box and threw its contents into the kitchen stove. Then, I was told by a neighbour, he stormed out of the house, swinging a bottle in each hand. He stayed away for three days, blind drunk in the middle of his grandfather's old woodlot.

❖ ❖ ❖

The days, the months that followed, were difficult for me. Lysandra withdrew into a secret self and refused to speak to me. She arrived at school late, never calling for me, and left the minute the bell rang, walk-running home with her huge eyes staring straight ahead. Twice I called for her at her house. The first time, her thin, sad mother answered the door, looked at me, and sighed. "She's not feeling well today, Elaine," she said. The other time, her father greeted me. "You!" he growled, and slammed the door. I didn't try again.

The long summer vacation passed, and I found other friends. Sometimes I would see Lysandra off in the distance, walking alone on the beach, or sitting on Rocky Point hugging her knees, eyes fixed on the water. But never writing. The weather, tired after a halcyon spring, turned rainy and chilly, but Lysandra still paced the shore, her hair blowing in the wet wind. Not fair, I thought. Twenty-three kids had entered that contest. It wasn't my fault that I won. Was it? Once I met her on the blueberry barrens. I had come up to get enough berries for Mom to make a pie. Lysandra was just sitting there on a granite boulder, hands limp in her lap.

"Lysandra," I pleaded. "It wasn't my fault."

"Wasn't it?" she said, eyes distant.

I looked hard at her, and noticed that she was pretty now, with a kind of wild gypsy beauty that didn't need fancy clothes or a trendy haircut.

"Lysandra. Please. Be nice again. I don't want our friendship to be wrecked."

"But it is," she said quietly.

"How can you do this to me for such a small thing?" I begged, not letting go.

"Small," she whispered. It was neither a question nor a

statement. Then she got down clumsily from the rock and walked out of the woods without looking back, picking her way carefully through the bushes and over the hummocks and outcroppings of stone.

I went home and cried for a while in my room. Then I picked up my wrinkled copy of the *South Shore Standard* and reread my poem. A part of me wanted to tear it into little pieces, press it all into a hard damp ball, and throw it at the wall. The other part folded it carefully and put it in my desk drawer. Then I grabbed my swimsuit off a hook and went down to the beach to go swimming with my other friends.

❖ ❖ ❖

Four years passed, and I was in grade 11. Grade 7 was long years behind me, and I scarcely noticed Lysandra as she came and went. Besides, my whole consciousness was absorbed by my feelings for Brett Houston. He had arrived fresh from the city of Toronto on the first day of school that year, and I had spent twenty-four weeks wanting him. As the year progressed, he had moved from pretty girl to pretty girl — in and out of our class — and I took courage from this fact. An early solid attachment, for instance, to the beauteous Sally Cornwall of grade 10, would have spelled permanence and hopelessness for me. But obviously he was still searching. Any minute it might be my turn.

And suddenly, miraculously, it was. Coming up behind me one day as I pulled books from my locker, he grabbed my arm and swung me around to face him. "Hi, cute stuff," he said in his wonderful flat Toronto voice. I looked at his size, his blond good looks, his casual grin, and my chest was alive with thundering heartbeats, tight with constricted breathing.

"Tonight," he said, moving his gum over to the other side of his mouth. "The movies. At eight. Time for a little ride first."

"Okay," I said, my hands shaking as they once again reached

for my books, my eyes only-marginally in focus.

"I'll walk you home," he said, slamming my locker door with a masterful bang.

Holy toledo, I thought.

❖ ❖ ❖

As the weeks went by, as March moved into April and then into May, I marvelled that this beautiful person was in my possession. Gone were the months of moving from girl to girl. We were going steady. It had lasted seven whole weeks. I waited on him, packed picnic lunches, wrote essays for him, massaged his shoulders after baseball practice, watched sports programs on TV all Saturday afternoon, mended his socks, walked his dog. Even I could see that I looked different, my skin aglow, my eyes eager, my smile at the ready. I adored him. I watched his coming and his going with undisguised worship.

I had a part-time job at a local variety store, and on the night of the Spring Dance, I had to work the evening shift. I told Brett I'd meet him at the school after the store closed at nine o'clock. He had to get there early to attach the balloons to the ceiling. When I entered the darkened gymnasium by the side door, I almost bumped into him. Him and Lysandra. They were facing one another, standing sideways to me. She had cut her hair in low bangs, and the rest of it hung almost to her waist, black as night. She had on large loop earrings and a low-cut black peasant blouse. There was a lot of chest to see, and her chest was a good one. That's all I remember about what she was wearing. I was too busy taking note of the way she was running a slender finger up and down his forearm, saying, "C'mon, Brett. Let's dance just a little bit while you're waiting. No point just standing around. She won't mind."

As they came together to dance a slow number, I watched that same finger move slowly up his spine and then come to rest on the back of his neck. She lifted her lovely face to his, enormous eyes mocking, ready. As she and Brett moved off in the darkness they looked like one person. They were dancing that close.

He came back and collected me. I'll say that for him. That evening we danced like mechanical dolls — arms and legs moving, but no life in us or between us. I could see Lysandra over by the springboards and the parallel bars, watching us, smiling. Brett waited until the next day to abandon me — without a word of explanation or farewell.

I thought I would die of heartbreak or wished I could, but of course I did nothing of the sort. Brett followed Lysandra around like a panting puppy all spring, servile, pliant, and sent her an orchid for the graduation formal. I went to that dance with Horace MacNab, who danced like a tractor, lumbering along, squashing my feet. I laughed loudly and frequently, tossing my hair over my shoulders. Brett and Lysandra glided around the gym with their eyes closed, slow-dancing to everything, their bodies pressed hard together.

The day after the formal, Lysandra told Brett she was tired of him and gave him back his baseball crest. Then she could be seen once again in the town library, reading, reading, and writing page after page of poetry. She had lost her stunned, vapid look. She moved once more with measured coordination, with grace. She even spoke to me from time to time — a neutral unadorned hello in passing.

Brett moved away with his family in the fall of that year. His father said he couldn't hack the climate. He said he wanted to live someplace where he could depend on owning a dry pair of shoes. I met Brett twenty years later at a high school reunion. He was thirty-eight years old, balding, stout, boring, a petulant wife in tow. Lysandra did not attend the reunion.

By now I've read a lot of Lysandra's poetry. It appears in academic journals and in the better popular magazines. She has published seven volumes and has won two national awards. She often turns up on the literary pages of newspapers, and I'm as likely to see her name in *The Globe and Mail* as in *The*

Halifax Mail-Star. The CBC loves to interview her. I don't understand many of her poems. They seem to be speaking a language that I never learned, and are plugged into a source of power that is a puzzle to me. But I can tell you this: her poetry contains such bitterness that the mind reels as it reads, dizzy from such savage images, such black revelations. The words claw out from the pages like so many birds of prey. And all of them seem to be moving in my direction.

MY MOTHER
AND FATHER

I WAS BORN IN GRACE Maternity Hospital in Halifax, entering the world noisily and with confidence, to greet a mother who was already a widow. Far from her home in the south of France, she spent eight solitary days in the hospital, and then wrapped me in a blue blanket and took me home to an empty house.

It was early November when we entered that house, and France must have seemed a hundred light-years away. My mother had come to Nova Scotia as a young war bride in 1919, and after ten childless years had finally given birth to her first and last baby. The next several months of my life in that home must have been terrible indeed for her. She and my father had moved from Wolfville to Halifax shortly before he died, and she was therefore living in a strange city as well as in a foreign land. Although she had an almost perfect mastery of English, she retained a slight French accent, and was considered strange, alien, too exotic for safety. As a result, she had few acquaintances, no close friends, and of course no husband. Furthermore, it would be six months before one could expect any semblance of summer to soften Canada's stern, uncompromising East Coast. It was fifteen years before I gave more than a few passing thoughts to these matters. Now I often think about them.

However, during my childhood I did think a great deal about my father. As a preschooler, I looked about me and noted that other houses contained fathers who left in the morning and returned at night. These same men took their children to the Halifax Exhibition, mended their tricycles, carried out the garbage, and put on the storm windows. "Where," I asked my mother, at age three, "is my father?" Long ago though that was, I can remember the scene well. She was washing the dishes at the time, and suddenly the sloshing and clatter stopped. I watched her as she stood silent and still, her wet hands clasping the edge of the sink. I even remember that she was wearing a black-and-white checked apron.

Finally, she shook her hands, dried them on the towel that was draped over her shoulder, and sat down beside me at the kitchen table. Her face was completely blank, telling me nothing. Taking my small hand in hers, she said, "Jeanne, my dear, I am sorry, but your father is dead." I asked if he would come back again, but she said no, he would not. Not ever. I thought about that, and then I went out to play. My mother returned to the dishes. I did not grieve or cry. There had been no face to love or miss, no presence to be significant by its absence. I simply lacked something I had never had — like a two-wheeled bike, a pet dog, or curly hair.

My mother maintained a silence on the subject of my father, and it was not until I started school that I asked any further questions. One day in the schoolyard, a small group of children lined up against the swings, chanting:

> "The girl in red
> Is a girl we know.
> She hasn't got a father.
> Ho! Ho! Ho!"

I was wearing a red coat; they were obviously referring to me. This nasty rhyme was a familiar one; I am sorry to say that I had already used it myself on other people. One day it might be:

"The girl in the reefer
Is a girl we know.
Her teeth are all crooked.
Ho! Ho! Ho!"

or one I remember forty years later with residual shame:

"The boy who smells
Is a boy we know.
His underwear is dirty.
Ho! Ho! Ho!"

When I returned home from school that noon, my mother was busy preparing dinner. We talked of this and that — unimportant friendly things. Yes, the spelling test was easy. No, I didn't want to take class piano lessons. Yes, I still liked my teacher very much. But I saved the important question until she was seated, fully occupied with nothing except me. I knew that my question was not a casual one.

As we settled down to our dinner of chicken and fried potatoes (I remember that very clearly), I spoke to her with no warning or preamble whatsoever. "How," I asked, as she raised her fork for the first bite, "did my father die?"

She lowered her fork slowly. She seemed to be thinking. Raising her left hand, she bit her thumbnail. Once again, there was no expression on her face. This was characteristic of her: you could never tell what she was thinking. Nowadays they talk a lot about people's vibrations — their vibes — and how we all should be alert to recognize and respond to them. My mother gave off no vibes. She had a masklike, expressionless face that registered love, but almost nothing else. This was both a good thing and a bad thing. I did not have to worry about her looking angry or worried. She never did. On the other hand, apart from what she actually said to me, I knew nothing about her whatsoever. She was a dutiful and in many ways a talented mother. She made me feel loved and secure; she also provided space and materials for creative and independent activities, encouragement for my efforts, interest in my life, and a consistent and dependable routine. But I had no idea who *she* was. Possibly this was fine, too. I *thought* I knew who she was: she was my mother.

I waited for her to reply. Then she pushed aside her fork and clasped her hands together in her lap.

"Your father," she said, "was a brave man. He fought for four years in the war and returned to Canada safe and sound." She sounded as though she were reciting a piece of prose as a school assignment. There was a singsong quality to her voice, and I could detect no feeling in it. "Ten years later, two months before you were born, we went for a picnic to Lawrencetown Beach. There had been a bad storm the previous day, and the waves were very high. A friend of his went in swimming, and was swept out to sea by the undertow. Your father swam out to try to save him, but the other man grabbed him and dragged him under the water. They both drowned." She then rose and dumped her entire untouched dinner into the garbage. "That," she said, her French accent suddenly very marked, "was the way it was." Then she added, "I hope this will not be making you in fear of the water."

No indeed, it would not be making me in fear of the water. Or of anything else, for that matter. I now had my father, and he would be at my side from then on, whenever I needed him. What I did not know about him I would invent. Unlike my mother, I hungrily attacked my dinner. With elation I gobbled down my chicken and my fried potatoes and asked for a second helping. Then I dashed out the back door, taking the short cut to school through a vacant lot. I knew exactly what I was going to do.

I waited until recess, and then I strode out to the swing set. In as loud a voice as I could muster, I chanted:

"The girl in red
Is a girl you know.
Her father was a *hero*.
Ho! Ho! Ho!"

It was the first time the rhyme had been used as a rebuttal. The children gathered around me, full of questions. What do you mean? What *kind* of hero? What did he *do*? I could see skepticism on some faces, grudging envy on others. So I told them my story — not without embellishment and flair. I did not have French ancestry for nothing. Gesticulating dramatically, I described the beach, the gigantic waves, the cries of the endangered friend. I told how my father, tall, strong, and magnificently built, tossed off his sweater and raced fearlessly into the raging seas, without a thought or backward glance. I lingered over the pursuit of the drowning man, speaking of the power of my father's swimming stroke, of his struggle with his friend, of the way the other man finally dragged him down to the cruel sea bottom. Looking about me, I could see that my audience was a receptive one. I then added a touching post-script, describing the scene on the shore, the sorrowing wives, the arrival of ambulances and stretchers, and the eventual funeral of that doomed heroic man.

From that day on, the vision of my father grew and flourished, and inside my head, he became taller and more handsome. His features were strong and firm, and he was gentle and brave at the same time. He did not lose his temper or scold, like Alena Marriot's father. He did not belch at the dinner table like Mr. Rankin, nor did he sit around on a deck chair on Sunday afternoons with a fat stomach hanging out. He did not have a fat stomach to begin with, and he also did not sit around. He was too busy taking me to circuses and on camping trips, fixing broken toys, and treating us to Popsicles and double deckers at the ice-cream store. He became my private prop, and I leaned on him often and confidently when the going was not smooth.

I talked a lot about this new father of mine at home. I described what he looked like, what he did, what kind of person he was. My mother listened passively, adding nothing, but also taking nothing away. When the summer months came, I would say to Mother, who had no car, "Dad would have taken us on picnics." When my swing set broke, I said to her, "My *father* could have fixed that." When I had difficulty with my math and she could not help me, I commented, "I'll bet *Dad* could have shown me how this worked." My father was as present in my life as if he had left at eight-thirty and would return again at six.

Gradually, as I started the perverse journey into my teens, I compared my mother more and more to my father and found her wanting. Why was she not more exciting? People from France are supposed to be passionate and fascinating. My father, who was only a *Canadian*, for heaven's sake, was *far* more interesting. Why didn't she have more friends, why couldn't she get rid of that accent, why didn't she buy a car? My father would have had a white convertible, and he would have been forever bringing his friends home for dinner, taking them out for drives, inviting them for the weekend. Why did my mother have to look so *drab*? Why did she pull her hair back from her face in a chignon, and why was she always dressed in black — black sweaters and black slacks, slim black skirts, simple little black dresses? I was tired of her perpetual single strand of pearls. My dad would have worn red plaid shirts on weekends and a blue sweatshirt for fishing. On formal occasions he would have sported a bright striped tie with his navy jacket and his grey flannels. There would have been variety and colour in his appearance.

My criticisms — spoken or silent — had little outward effect on my mother, except to make her a little more quiet, a little more sad. This was worse than the still and mysterious dignity that I was used to, and it infuriated me. I did not want to hurt her. I even loved her. But what I really wanted was for her to change. Why couldn't she? Or why *wouldn't* she? I couldn't understand it. To me it seemed so simple. I had pointed out to her the flaws that marred her image to me and to the world. Why did she not at least *argue*? I wanted a mother who was lively, passionate, responsive. I looked at her carefully, objectively. She was very pretty. Her features were small, regular, and well defined; her eyes were enormous. Her hair was thick and still black. In my mind, I refashioned her. Closing my eyes, I put her in a fiery red dress; I curled her hair; I had her dance a jig in the living room. But when I opened my eyes she was still there, features composed, sitting quietly, knitting a pair of argyle socks for her brother in France. She looked up at me and asked gently, "Would you like fish or meat patties for supper?"

I sighed. "Fish," I replied, and went upstairs to finish my homework. The click of her knitting needles got on my nerves.

One Saturday in 1944, when I was a brittle tense fifteen years of age, I woke up at 8:00 A.M. and contemplated the coming day. I would call my best friend, Judy, and arrange to go shopping with her in the afternoon; later, we would have Cokes at the counter in Diana Sweets, and talk about school and life and boys. Jerry McInnis and his friends might be there, too, and someone might ask us to the Hi-Y dance. I jumped out of bed and started dressing. Clothed in bra and panties, I scrutinized myself in the mirror. Not great, I thought, but not bad. My figure was slim but not shapeless. I had small, firm breasts, a tiny waist, and tidy hips. Built like my mother, I thought wryly. I had a lot of jet-black hair; a Veronica Lake hairstyle covered one-half of my small white face. I looked at myself and the world out of one eye.

Enough of this, I thought, and poked around in my bureau for my stockings. These were pre-jeans days. If you wanted to cut a dash in Diana Sweets or on Barrington Street or in Mills

Brothers clothing store, you wore a pleated skirt, a baggy
sweater, and stockings. It was still wartime, and nylons were
non-existent except through something called the black mar-
ket; panty hose had yet to be invented. But we did have
stockings that were less utilitarian than lisle ones, and I
searched feverishly for what I knew was my last pair. I opened
drawer after drawer and suddenly remembered that I had torn
them last week on that stupid broken chair rung. Dad would
have fixed that long ago, I thought savagely. He was dead, and
my mother was no good at fixing things, and I couldn't go
downtown without stockings, and I was furious. I stalked into
my mother's room and stared at her bureau drawers. I could
hear her downstairs moving about in the kitchen, and I felt
that I was safe. I would have done bodily injury to anyone who
so much as touched my dresser drawers but I coldly and
systematically explored drawer after drawer, in my search for
a pair of stockings that I could steal. It was as though I were
thinking, If you can't provide me with a father, at least supply
me with some stockings.

At last I found the right drawer. It was very small, and it was
in a night table that I would not have expected to hold clothing.
The drawer contained about five pairs, and I looked them over
in order to consider size, shade, texture. Underneath the
stockings was a small envelope on which was written "PRI-
VATE." I opened it without hesitation.

Inside the envelope were seven photographs. There was one
snapshot of a little girl with long black hair and a big grin,
hamming it up for the camera in an extravagant pose. Was it
me, or was it my mother? She looked like both of us; but this
picture was yellow and old. There was another shot of a young
woman in a long white dress; she was small, radiant, and very
elegant. Her hair was pulled back from her exquisite little face,
and she held herself like a duchess. I knew who *she* was. Next
came a studio portrait of a young man. Apart from an expression of almost oppressive cheerfulness, he was singularly un-

attractive. He had pale eyes, a poorly defined chin, and a lot
of over-large teeth. I wondered if this was the brother for
whom she knitted those complicated argyle socks. Probably,
because he was in each of the next three pictures. I picked them
up one by one. The first showed my mother and him standing
on the deck of a ship. They were laughing, and they looked
very happy. His hat was off, and his thin wispy hair was blowing
every which way, doing nothing to improve his indifferent
features. The next picture was of him alone, standing on a
beach in an old-fashioned bathing suit. His shoulders were
narrow, his thin hair was plastered down on his head and parted
in the middle, and his knees were nobbly. Then there was a
snapshot of him in uniform, saluting in an exaggerated military
manner, grinning into the camera. Silly, I thought. No wonder
my mother had never bothered to visit her brother.

The sixth picture was like a physical blow to me. I looked
at it for a full minute before I was ready to accept its significance. My mother, still radiant, was standing in the centre of
the picture, dressed once more in the elegant white dress. She
held a large bouquet of flowers. Beside her, looking at her and
thus revealing to the camera his unfortunate chin line, was the
same man. He stood perhaps half an inch taller than my
mother. To the left were a middle-aged man and woman; to
the right was a young couple in formal dress.

If indeed this was a wedding picture, and it certainly was,
my mother had married that seedy-looking little stranger. And
if she had married him, he was my father.

I tried to absorb the enormity of my discovery. Frantically
my mind clutched at the vision of my tall, imposing father —
compassionate, dependable. But apparently he was not, after
all, either compassionate or dependable, because he was already fading. As I stood there in my mother's bedroom, dressed
only in my underwear and my garter belt, he bade me a dim
farewell. In his place stood this terrible man, this wispy inter-
loper with too many teeth. Numb shock gave way to fury, and

grabbing the pictures, I slammed the drawer shut and fled to my room. My mind was a confusion of swiftly revolving wheels, interlocking, relentlessly turning. I could focus on nothing. As I dressed, I stole anxious looks in the mirror, looking for signs of my new parentage. I inspected my eyes, my chin line, my mouth, my hair, even my shoulders. It was all right. I was entirely my mother's child. Evidently my father's genes had made no mark upon me. Having no stockings (who cared?) I ripped off my garter belt and pulled on sweater, skirt, socks, and saddle shoes. Savagely I brushed my hair, stopping periodically to inspect that insipid stranger who had sent my real father away. My wheels turned and turned and found no track. My wrath was terrible, but I could not centre it. My mother's husband, as I chose to think of him, received his share. How *dared* he be my father, presenting to me his unwelcome inheritance, hiding for all those years and then appearing among my mother's stockings to mock me, evicting my real father. Some of my rage was directed at that imaginary father, too — for not existing, for leaving me to this dead and un- attractive man, for betraying me. And my mother: my anger mounted, and my heart pounded against my rib cage. How could she have let me live this lie for so long? I stalked out of the room and prepared to join battle in the kitchen.

When I entered the room, my mother was making pancakes at the far counter, and her back was to me. She turned around and welcomed me with her gentle smile, which abruptly faded. I made up for my mother's lack of vibrations. Even in those days before the invention of vibes, I vibrated with an intensity that was unmistakable. On that morning, a blind person, a deaf-mute, would have known that something was wrong.

"What is wrong, Jan?" asked my mother, who had long ago adopted the English version of my French name. She waited, still and impassive, for my answer.

I slammed the pictures down on the kitchen counter beside the mixing bowl. I swung around and faced her, pointing a shaking finger at the little pile of photographs. "What's wrong?" I cried, "What's *wrong*! *Everything's* wrong! My whole *life* is wrong! Who is that *man*? That awful *man*? Why is he my father? How could you hide these things for so long? How could you *do* this to me?" I searched in my mind for the comfort of my former father. But he had departed, and I was alone. I pounded the table, the counter, and then clutched both sides of my head. Absurdly I shouted, "What have you done with my father?"

My mother watched me, her face unreadable. She wiped her hands on her apron. She took it off. She looked at me in silence for a few moments. Then she picked up an empty bottle from the counter and hurled it against the opposite wall, smashing it into countless pieces. My tempest stilled as quickly as if she had fired a rifle into the air, and I watched her, transfixed, my wheels stopped and still and waiting.

"How dare you!" She spoke at first quietly, through her teeth, and then gradually her voice gathered force and volume. "How dare you," she repeated savagely, "open my private drawer and put your nosy little self-centred hands on my past?" She had never spoken to me like this before. Never. "How dare you," she went on, "pass judgement on my choice of husband or his merits? You who have lived with a cardboard father for these nine long years. What do you know about pain or about patience or about the need to hold your tongue?"

There was a pause, while she caught her breath. I was too stunned to be frightened, too fascinated to be quiet. "But why didn't you *tell* me?" I pleaded.

"Why didn't I tell you?" She had found her breath, and was launched once more upon her defence. It was as though she could speak forever, as though the bottle, when it broke, had released the locked-up voice and pain of fifteen years. "Because *you* told *me*. You told me who he was, what he looked like, the nature of his personality." As she continued, her French accent intensified, fracturing her impeccable and bloodless English,

revealing the passion behind her words. Sometimes she retained her *th*'s, sometimes not. Her sentences were convoluted
and peppered with French words. "What was I to be doing?"
she asked, throwing her arms wide. "You were loving this
figure *du papier* long before you ever made mention of his
existence. I have known always that a child need two parents,
and you seemed to be so happy with this nothing-man you
made into your *papa*. He seemed to make you strong even, to
make you think we were a family *complète*, not just *toi et moi*.
Mon Dieu! Do you think I wanted this stranger in our house?"
She was pacing the kitchen now like a panther in a cage, back
and forth, around, across. She pointed, spread her arms,
pounded her fists on the counter. "But when he was presented
to me, this *étranger*, this *inconnu*, you were too young, I
thought, too fragile, to disappoint. He was the big hero, the
Superman of your life, and what is more, all your friends were
believing the reality of this big lie. How could I take him away
from you? So I hid your father under my stockings, where I
assumed" — she raised her lovely chin and looked at me sideways — "I assumed that nobody would have the very bad
breeding to be going."

"Oh, *Maman*!" I said, slipping oddly, naturally, into my
childhood name for her, reaching out to touch her as she swept
by. "What was he, the *real* he, really like?"

"Just one little moment!" she cried, still pacing. "I have not
even begin to finish. I have to tell you how I hate this cardboard
father of yours. I let him live here because you need him, but
I feel many times like I could kill him dead. He was always
better than me. More exciting. *Plus vivant. Plus beau.* Me, I was
the silent one, the dull one. I could not fix the bicycles, the
chairs. It is a very bad thing to be jealous. But to be jealous of
a person who do not even exist is an agony. And a mother," she
added bleakly, "loves very hard."

"Come on, *Maman*," I coaxed, rising and taking her hand,
stopping her pacing. "Please. I'm ready now. I'm even sorry.

Tell me. Tell me about your husband."

She sat down then. She looked more like her old composed self. "I was seventeen," she said, "and it was France and the war, and *même s'il faisait* very warm and sunny, it was a time of fear and hunger, too. Then came this soldier man, an *officier* even, and me so young, and he came from a land so far away, and it was a romantic thing. You think he does not look so handsome like your paper father, but he was not so bad as he look in the pictures. He was very fun and always laughing, and *un peu* reckless, you know, and not afraid of things. Or seemed like that. Now I wonder. I think maybe he was afraid of so much that he had to prove things all the time. He got medals in the war. I even think now that maybe I was one of his medals, his trophies. It was a reckless thing to bring back to Canada — *English* Canada — a French wife. But I was unique. I was pretty, I was *chic*. He could say, 'Look. I am not tall or handsome or even very clever. But I have capture this young girl along with my medals, and she is the only one exactly like herself. She is special. So maybe *I* am, too.' And *souvent* I think that people believed him."

There was a silence. She was sitting quietly now, staring sadly into space. I felt I should say something — something kind. "And what about the drowning?" I asked gently. "I guess he was a hero after all."

She rose swiftly and continued her pacing. "A hero!" she cried scornfully. "What makes a hero? A hero is living with your own bad things and staring them in the face. That beach and that drowning I will never forgive. *Never*. To begin with, you do not take a seven-month pregnant wife and friends with four tiny children to a beach in a raging wind when everyone know the beach is dangerous. But no. He want to go, so we all go. I learn very early that what he say, we do. Then the foolish other man go to swim in that terrible sea, because your father *dare* him to go. He call him a coward if he do not go. So he start to drown. And what do my husband do? There are other people on the beach, some of them big men, and life preservers on a pole. There is even a boat not far away. But no. This so reckless man just jump in the water and be the big hero to save his friend, who is twice as big as he is. He leave on shore his wife and his unborn child, and the other woman and her four children. Not one of us could swim. Not one. And we have to stand there and watch it all happening. I won't tell you all the bad parts, but how you like to be those little children and see their daddy brought in dead by the other men? Stupid! Stupid! I can never forgive it!"

And my mother sat down and put her face into her hands and cried like a child. I picked up my chair and took it over beside her. I put my arms around her and hugged her and let her cry and cry. She had fifteen years of crying to do, and I was in no rush to stop her. My frozen mother had thawed, and there was no way I was going to interrupt the process.

Finally, she stopped crying, and gazed at me, red-eyed. She seemed to have regained her mastery of English. "I'm sorry," she said, "that I wouldn't try to change, to make you proud of me. But I had put the rest of myself in a box and pulled down the lid. I refused to change my hair and my clothes, too. And," she added. "I still do."

"*Maman*," I said, my throat tight, "I'm sorry. You're beautiful. *Comme tu es belle*." And strangely, I believed it. I looked at her sad, distinguished little face with its lovely bones, enhanced by the simplicity of her hair. I admired her trim figure in her tasteful little black dress. "My dad was right," I said. "You *were* special. One of a kind. A real trophy."

We talked for a long time that day. The years fell away, and she seemed young again — animated, released, a person as well as a mother. I moved out of childhood, and put one foot into the adult world.

As for my mother, she took off her apron and accepted a job as translator in a government department. Discovering French-Canadian women who were strangers in Halifax, she befriended them, making them feel welcome in a chilly environment. At the age of fifty, *Maman* met and married a Québécois university teacher, and went to live in Montreal. At seventy-eight, he is a lively and sensitive person, warm, sophisticated, and a good father to me. My mother's hair is white now, but still thick, and she wears it drawn back from her lovely old face in a chignon. She stands proud, erect, and her figure, in her simple black dresses, is still slender. She nearly always wears a single strand of pearls.

THE
LEAVING

SHE TOOK ME WITH HER the day she left. "Where y' goin', Ma?" I asked. She was standing beside my bed with her coat on.

"Away," said Ma. "And yer comin', too."

I didn't want to go anywhere. It was three o'clock in the morning, and I was warm in my bed.

"Why me?" I complained.

I was too sleepy to think of any more complicated questions. In any case, there were no choices and very few questions back then when we were kids. You went to school and you came home on the school bus. If your father wanted you to shovel snow or fetch eggs, he told you, and you did it. He didn't ask. He told. Same with Ma. I did the dishes and brought in the firewood when it was required. She just pointed to the sink or to the woodbox, and I would leave whatever I was doing and start work. But at 3:00 a.m., the situation seemed unusual enough to permit a question. Therefore I asked again, "Why me?"

"Because yer the smartest," she said. "And because yer a woman."

I was twelve years old that spring.

❖ ❖ ❖

Ma was a tall, rangy woman. She had a strong handsome face, with high cheekbones and a good firm chin line. Her lips were full. Her teeth were her own, although she smiled so rarely that you seldom saw them; her mouth tended to be held in a set straight line. She did not exactly frown; it was more as though she were loosely clenching her teeth. Her eyes were veiled, as if she had shut herself off from her surroundings and was thinking either private thoughts or nothing at all. Oh, she was kind enough and gentle enough when we needed it, though perhaps we needed it more often than she knew. But when we had cut knees or tonsillectomies, or when friends broke our hearts, she would hold us and hug us. Her mouth would lose its hard tight shape, and her eyes would come alive with concern and love.

Her lovely crisp auburn hair was short and unshaped making her face look uncompromising and austere. She wore baggy slacks over her excellent legs, and she owned two shabby grey sweaters and two faded graceless blouses. I did not ask myself why my mother looked this way, or why she had retreated behind her frozen face. One accepts one's parents for a long time, without theory or question. Speculation comes later, with adolescence and all the uncertainty and confusion it brings.

But when she woke me that chilly May morning, I was still a child. I rose and dressed quickly, packing my school bag with my pyjamas and toothbrush, the book I was reading, a package of gum, the string of Woolworth pearls that my grandmother had given me on my tenth birthday, and some paper to write and draw on. I wore jeans, my favourite blue sweater, my winter jacket, and rubber boots. I forgot my hat.

My mother had told me to be quiet, so I slithered down the stairs without a single board creaking. She was waiting at the door, holding a black cardboard suitcase with a strap around it. A shopping bag held sandwiches and some of last fall's bruised apples. She wore a brown car coat over her black slacks, and her hair was hidden under a grey wool kerchief. Her mouth had its tense fixed look, but her eyes were alive. Even at my age and at that hour, I could see that.

We stopped briefly before walking out into the cold night air. The stove in the kitchen was making chugging noises, and from different parts of the small house could be heard a variety of snores and heavy breathing. My four brothers and my father were not going to notice our departure.

For a moment, my mother seemed to hesitate. Her mouth softened, and a line deepened between her eyebrows. Then she straightened her shoulders and opened the door. "Move!" she whispered.

We stepped into the night and started walking down the mountain in the direction of town, six miles away. I did not quarrel with the need for this strange nocturnal journey, but I did question the reason.

"Ma," I said.

She turned and looked at me.

"Ma. Why are we leavin'?"

She didn't answer right away. It crossed my mind that she might not be sure of the reason herself. This was a frightening thought. But apparently she knew.

"I plans t' do some thinkin'," she said.

We walked quickly through the night. North and South Mountains closed off the sky behind us and far ahead, but a full moon made it easy to see our way on the frosty road. The hill country was full of scrub growth, stubby spruce, and sprawling alders, unlike the tidy fields and orchards of the Valley. But the frost lent a silver magic to the bushes and the rough ground, and the moonlight gave a still dignity to the shabby houses. It was cold, and I shivered. "Fergot yer hat," said Ma. "Here." She took the warm wool kerchief from her head and gave it to me. I took it. Parents were invincible, and presumably would not feel the cold. My mother was not a complainer. She was an endurer. It was 1969, and she was forty-five years old.

When we reached Annapolis, we stopped at a small house

on the edge of town, and Ma put down her suitcase and dug around in her purse. She took out a key and opened the door. Even my silent mother seemed to think that an explanation was required. "Lida Johnson's in Glace Bay, visitin' her daughter. Said I could use the house while she's gone. Normie's at a 4-H meetin' in Bridgetown. Joseph's truckin'. We'll wait here till th' train goes."

"Ma," I asked, "how long we gonna be gone?"

She bent her head down from its rigid position and looked at the floorboards of the front hall. She touched her mouth briefly with her fist. She closed her eyes for a second and took a deep breath.

"Dunno," she replied. "Till it's time."

❖ ❖ ❖

We slept in the parlour until we left for the station.

I guess that six-mile walk had shunted me straight from childhood into adolescence, because I did an awful lot of thinking between Annapolis and Halifax. But at first I was too busy to think. I was on a train, and I had never been inside one before. There were things to investigate — the tiny washroom with its little sink, and the funny way to flush the toilet. In the main part of the Dayliner, the seats slid up and down so that people could sleep if they wanted to. I watched the world speed by the windows — men working on the roads; kids playing in schoolyards; cows standing dumbly outside barns in the chilly air, all facing in the same direction; places and towns I had never seen till then. My ma looked over at me and placed a comic book and a bag of peanuts on my lap. "Fer th' trip," she said, and smiled, patting my knee in an unfamiliar gesture. "Mind missin' school?" she added.

"No," I said. But I did. I had a part in the class play, and there was a practice that afternoon. I was the chief fairy, and I had twenty-five lines, all of which I knew by heart already. But this trip was also a pretty special, if alarming, adventure. It had a beginning but no definite end, and we were still speeding toward the middle. What would Halifax be like? We never had enough money to have more than one ride on the Exhibition ferris wheel at Lawrencetown; but here we were buying train tickets and reading comics and eating peanuts and travelling to heaven knows what expensive thrills.

"Maw," I asked, "where'd the money come from?"

She looked at me, troubled.

"Don't ask," she said. "I'll tell you when you're eighteen."

Eighteen! I might as well relax and enjoy myself. But I wondered.

Before long, she fell asleep, and I felt free to think. Until then, it was almost as though I were afraid she would read my thoughts.

Why had we left? How long would we be gone? How would Pa and my brothers cook their dinner? How would they make their beds? Who would they complain to after a hard day? Who would fetch the eggs, the mail, the water, the wood, the groceries? Who would wash their overalls, mend their socks, put bandages on their cuts? It was inconceivable to me that they could survive for long without us.

❖ ❖ ❖

When we reached Halifax, we went to what I now realize was a cheap and shabby hotel in the South End of the city. But to me it seemed the height of luxury. The bed was made of some kind of shiny yellow wood. The bedspread was an intense pink, with raised nubbles all over it. A stained spittoon sat in the corner. There was actually a sink in the room, with taps that offered both cold and hot water. A toilet that flushed was down the hall. I checked under the bed; there was no chamber pot. But who needed it? There were two pictures on the walls — one of a curly-headed blonde, displaying a lot of bare flesh, and another of three dead ducks hanging upside down from a nail. I spent a lot of time inspecting both of these pictures.

Halifax was a shock to me. How could the buildings be so huge and the stores so grand? Here I was in the province's capital city before I really understood what a capital city could be. I admired the old stone buildings with their carvings around the doors and windows. I stretched my neck to see the tops of the modern apartments, with their glass and concrete reaching up into the clouds. The buses and cars alarmed me as they rushed up and down the long streets, but they excited me, too. The weather changed; it was warm and comforting, and the wind was gentle and caressing. We went down the hill to the harbour, and saw the bridge; rooted in the ground and in the sea bottom, it lifted its enormous metal wings into the sky. I marvelled that a thing so strong could be so graceful, so beautiful. What a lovely way, I thought, to get from one place to another. We walked across the bridge to Dartmouth, and watched the ships, far below, headed for Europe, for Africa, for the distant North. My mother, who had started to talk, told me about all these things. It was as though she were trying to tell me something important, but didn't want to say things right out. "They're goin' somewheres," she said. Later on, she took me out to Dalhousie University, and we walked among the granite buildings and beside the playing fields. "If yer as smart as the teacher claims," she said, "maybe you'll come here some day t' learn." I thought this highly unlikely. If we couldn't afford running water, how could we afford such a thing as that? I said so.

"They's ways," she said.

We walked up and down Spring Garden Road and gazed in the big windows. I looked at a candy store with at least five million kinds of candy, shops with dresses so fancy that I could scarcely believe it, shelves full of diamonds and gold and sparkling crystal. "Is there ways for all this, too?" I asked my mother. She hesitated.

"Don't need all that stuff," she concluded.

The weather was dazzling — a sunny Nova Scotia May day.

We walked through the huge iron gates into the Public Gardens and ate our sandwiches and apples beside the duck pond. I kicked off my rubber boots and wiggled my toes in the sun as I watched the swans and the yellow ducklings. The Gardens were immense, full of massive and intricate flowerbeds, winding paths, and strange exotic trees. There were statues, a splashing fountain, an elaborate round bandstand, and a little river with a curved bridge over it. Lovers strolled arm in arm, and children shrieked with laughter as they chased the pigeons. I asked Ma why everyone seemed so happy. "Dunno," she said. "Weather does things t' people." She looked around. "And maybe some of them's free," she added.

On the second day, we watched women racing to work in the morning, mini-skirts flipping, heels clicking, faces eager, faces tense. We looked on as shopping women pulled twenty-dollar bills out of their purses as though they were nickels. We saw the drunks sleeping on the pavement outside the mission. We visited the courthouse and looked at the pictures of the stern-faced judges as they watched us from the walls. "They fixes things what aren't right," said Ma. I wondered how. "But not always," she added.

We spent an hour in the public library, looking at the shelves and shelves of books, smelling their wonderful book smells, idly turning the pages. On a book dolly, she picked up a copy of *The Feminine Mystique*. She, who had not to my knowledge read a single book since I was born, said shyly, "I read this book." I was astonished.

"You!" I exclaimed. "How come? When?"

"I kin read!" she retorted, miffed. "Even if y' leaves school in grade 5, y' kin read. Y' reads slow, but y' knows how."

"But where'd you get it?" I demanded, amazed.

"Y' remember that day the Salvation Army lady brought us that big box o' clothes?" she asked. "Yer pa was mad and said we didn't need no charity. But I hid the box, and after a time he forgot about it. Well, there was other things in there, too —

an egg beater, some toys what I gave to Lizzie's kids, even a string o' yellow beads and a bracelet that I bin savin' fer you. And some books. There was comic books and that big colourin' book y' got fer Christmas, and them *Popular Mechanics* magazines the boys read, and a coupla others. And this." She placed the palm of her hand on the book. "Seemed like it was for me, special. So I read it. She was real tough goin', but I read every word. Took me near a year. Finished it last Thursday."

I could hardly believe it. My ma didn't even read recipes. She kept them all in her head. I asked, "Was it good?"

She thought for a moment before answering. "She was a real troublin' book. But she was good."

I couldn't understand that. "If it was so troublin', why was it so good?"

She answered that one without hesitation. "Found I weren't alone," she said. She stroked its cover tenderly before putting it back on the dolly. I liked the library, with all the silent people bent over their books, and the librarians moving soundlessly to and fro. I wasn't used to quiet places.

In the afternoon, we climbed the Citadel and went into its museum, walking up and down among the sea things, old things, rich things. Later on, we went to what I thought was a very fancy restaurant. There were bright, shiny chrome tables with place mats of paper lace and green glass ashtrays. I ordered a hot dog and chips, because that was my favourite meal. My mother, her mouth now soft and cheerful, ordered something with a strange name.

"Ain't gonna come all this way and spend all th' hen money jest t' eat what I kin eat at home," she said.

The egg money! So that was it. I let on I didn't notice. But a thrill of fear ran through me. I wondered what Pa would do.

In the evening we returned early to the hotel, and I slept deeply, but with strange and troubled dreams.

❖ ❖ ❖

On the third day, Ma said, "It's time. T'day we go home." I asked why.

"Because," she said.

"Because why?" I insisted.

She was silent for a moment, and then said again, "It's time." I was pleased. It had been an interesting trip, but it frightened me a little because there were no explanations, no answers to my unspoken questions. Besides, I was afraid that someone else would get to be chief fairy in the school play. "Have you done yer thinkin'?" I asked. She looked at me strangely. There was hope in her look and an odd fierce dignity.

"I has," she said.

❖ ❖ ❖

We took the bus home instead of the train, and it was late afternoon when we arrived in Annapolis to start the six-mile climb to our farm. The day was damp and cold, and I wore my mother's wool kerchief again. We were very quiet, and I knew she was nervous. Her mouth was back in its taut line, and her eyes were troubled. But even in the wind, her shoulders were straight and firm, and I could feel a difference in her. Fearful though her eyes were, she was fully alert, and you could sense a new dogged strength in the set of her face.

There was no such strength in me, except such as I derived from her. Home is home when you are twelve, and I did not want to live a tourist's life in Halifax forever. But I worried every step of the six long miles.

As we turned the bend at Harrison's Corner, we could see the farm in the distance. It was as though I were seeing it for the first time. The house had been white once, but it had needed paint for almost nineteen years. Around the yard was a confusion of junk of all kinds: two discarded cars — lopsided and without wheels — an unpiled jumble of firewood, buckets, a broken hoe, rusty tools, an old oil drum for burning garbage. To the left were the few acres of untidy fields, dotted with spruce trees and the grey skeletons of trees long dead of Dutch elm disease. To the right, close to the henhouse, was the barn — small and unpainted, grey and shabby in the dim afternoon light. We could hear the two cows complaining, waiting for milking time.

When we opened the kitchen door, they were all there. My four big brothers were playing cards at the table, and my father was sitting by the kitchen stove, smoking a cigarette and drinking from a bottle of beer. I had forgotten how darkly handsome he was. But because it was not Sunday, he was unshaven, and his eyes glared out at us from beneath heavy black eyebrows.

Pa rose from his chair and faced us. He was very tall, and his head almost reached the low ceiling. He seemed to fill the entire room. He crushed out his cigarette on the top of the stove.

His voice was low and threatening. "Where you bin, woman?" he said.

She spoke, and I was amazed that she had the courage. Then I realized with a jolt that his words were little different in tone and substance from hundreds I had heard before: "How come my supper's not ready, woman?" "Move smart, woman! I'm pressed fer time!" "Shut up them damn kids, woman!" "Move them buckets, woman! They're in my way!" "This food ain't fit t' eat, woman. Take it away!"

She spoke quietly and with dignity. "You is right to be angry, Lester," she said. "I left a note fer y', but I shoulda tole y' before I left."

"Shut yer mouth, woman, and git my supper!" he shouted, slamming the beer bottle down on the table.

She moved to the centre of the room and faced him. "My name," she began, and faltered. She cleared her throat and ran her tongue over her lower lip. "My name," she repeated, this time more steadily, "is Elizabeth."

He was dumbfounded. My brothers raised their heads from

their card game and waited, cards poised in midair.

Pa looked at her. He looked at me. Then he looked at Jem and Daniel and Ira and Bernard, sitting there silent and still like four statues, waiting for his reaction.

Suddenly my father threw back his head and laughed. His ugly laughter filled the little kitchen, and we all listened, frozen, wishing for it to stop.

" 'My name is Elizabeth!' " he mocked, between choking guffaws, slapping his thighs and holding his stomach, and then he repeated himself and her, mincingly, " 'My . . . name . . . is . . . Elizabeth!' " Then his face changed, and there was silence. "Git over here 'n' make my supper, woman! I'm gonna milk them cows. But my belly is right empty, and y' better be ready when I gits back from th' chores!"

I watched my mother. During the laughter, I could see her retreat for a minute behind her eyes, expressionless, lifeless, beaten. Then she took a deep breath and looked at him directly, squarely, with no fear in her face. Pain, yes, but no fear. My brothers looked down and continued their card game.

"Act smart there, Sylvie," she said to me, as soon as he had left. "I need yer help bad. You clean up, 'n' I'll fix supper." She was already moving swiftly about the kitchen, fetching food, chopping onions, peeling potatoes.

In the sink was a mountainous pile of dirty dishes. Open cans, crusted with stale food, cluttered the counter. I surveyed the scene with distaste.

"Ma," I asked, complaining like the true adolescent that I had now become, "how come they couldna washed the dishes themselves? They goes huntin' and fishin' and has lotsa little vacations in th' winter. We always do their work for them when they're gone. How come we gotta clean up their mess?"

"Listen," she said, cutting the potatoes and dropping them into the hot fat, "the way I sees it is y' kin ask fer kindness or politeness from time t' time. But y' can't expect no miracles. It's my own fault fer raisin' four boys like they was little men.

I shoulda put them in front of a dishpan fifteen years ago. Now it's too late. Yer pa's ma did the same thing. She aimed t' raise a boy who was strong and brave, with no soft edges." She wiped her forehead with the back of her hand. "All along I bin blamin' men fer bein' men. But now I see that oftentimes it's the women that makes them that way." It was a long, long speech for my ma. But she went on. "The boys is seventeen, eighteen, nineteen and twenty years old. Y' can't start makin' 'em over now. They're set." Then she smiled wryly, with a rare show of humour. She bowed formally in the direction of the card game. "I apologizes," she said, "to your future wives."

Then she stopped, and looked from one son's face to the next, and so on, around the table. "I loves you all, regardless," she said softly, "and it's worth a try. Jem" — she spoke to the youngest — "I'd be right grateful if you'd fetch some water for Sylvie. She's real tired after the long walk."

Jem looked at his brothers, and then he looked at her. Water carrying was woman's work, and she knew she was asking a lot of him. He rose silently, took the bucket from her, and went outside to the well.

"And you," she said, addressing Daniel and Ira and Bernard, "One snigger out of you, and yer in bad trouble." I'm sure she knew she was taking an awful chance. You can say a thing like that to little boys, but these were grown men. But no one moved or so much as smiled when Jem returned. "I thank you right kindly," said Ma, thereby delivering a speech as unusual as her other one.

❖ ❖ ❖

You could say, I suppose, that our leaving made no large difference in my mother's life. She still worked without pay or praise, and was often spoken to as though she were without worth or attraction. Her days were long and thankless. She emptied chamber pots and spittoons, scrubbed overalls and sheets on her own mother's scrub board, and peeled the frozen clothes from the line in winter with aching fingers. But not all things remained the same. She now stood up to my father. Her old paralytic fear was gone, and she was able to speak with remarkable force and dignity. She did not nag. Nagging is like a constant blow with a small blunt instrument. It annoys, but it seldom makes more than a small dent. When she chose to object to Pa's cruel or unfair behaviour, her instrument was a shining steel knife with a polished cutting edge. A weapon like that seemed to make my father realize that if he went too far — if he beat her, or if he scolded too often or too unjustly — she would leave. After all, she had done it once before. And this time, she might not return.

So there were changes. One day, for no apparent reason, he started to call her Elizabeth. She did not let on that this was remarkable, but the tight line of her mouth relaxed, and she made him a lemon pie for supper. She fixed up the attic storeroom as a workroom for herself. The boys lugged up her treadle sewing machine, and she brought in an old wicker chair and a table from the barn. It was a hot room in summer and cold in winter, but it was her own place — her escape. She made curtains from material bought at Frenchy's, and hooked a little rug for the floor. No one was allowed to go there except her. She always emerged from this room softer, gentler, more still.

I never did hear a single word about the missing egg money. Maybe Pa didn't notice, or perhaps Ma attacked the subject with her sharp-edged knife. Possibly it was the egg money that sent me to Dalhousie — that and my scholarship and my summer jobs. I never asked. I didn't really want to know.

When I was home last February during the term break, I stole a look into Ma's attic room. There were library books on the table, material on the sewing machine, paper piled on the floor for her letters to me and to the boys. I respected her privacy and did not go in. But the room, even in that chilly winter attic, looked like an inviting place.

My ma is now fifty-five, and has a lot of life still to live. My pa is fifty-eight. He still shaves once a week, and he has not yet cleared up the yard. But he often speaks to my mother as though she were more of a person and less of a thing. Sometimes he says thank-you. He still has a raging temper, but he is an old dog, and new tricks come hard. He loves my mother and she him, with a kind of love that is difficult for my generation to understand or define. In another time and in another place, the changes could have been more marked. But my mother is a tough and patient woman, and these differences seem to be enough for her. Her hair is worn less severely. Her mouth is not set so straight and cold and firm. She talks more. She has made a pretty yellow blouse to wear with her baggy slacks. She smiles often, and she is teaching her two grandsons how to wash dishes and make cookies.

I often wonder about these things: but when my mind approaches the reasons for all that has happened, my thinking slides away and my vision blurs. Certainly the book and the leaving do not explain everything. Maybe my mother was ready to move into and out of herself anyway; and no one can know exactly what went on in her thoughts before and after she left. Perhaps she was as surprised as I was by the amount of light and warmth she let in when she opened the door to step into the dark and frosty morning. But of that strange three-day departure, I can say, as Ma did of her book, "She was a real troublin' trip. But she was good."

MY COUSIN
CLARETTE

Toronto, 1984. SCENE, the Dundas station of the Yonge Street subway. Time, about 11:00 A.M. Hanging back as usual, loath to fall onto that track in front of an oncoming train, I leaned against the wall, my arms full of packages and shopping bags. Not so the lady in front of me. She stood in her high-heeled boots at the edge of the platform, erect, confident. From the back, I admired her crisp blond hair, styled short and simply; I envied her navy blue suede coat, perfectly cut, her long leather boots. I marvelled that she could be returning home without a single parcel to clutter her image — on December 20th. A shoulder bag, the cost of which I assessed down to the last cent, hung on her left shoulder. Exactly the way I would like to look after a pre-Christmas trip downtown. All her parcels sent home by courier, I mused. Neither delay nor cost would bother that woman. I inched forward gingerly, on the pretense of looking for the train, already late, and stole a glance at her profile. I wanted to see if the front view was worthy of the back. Half hoping to find a face less perfect than the rest of her — acne on the chin perhaps, or a pair of thick telescope glasses — I peered more intently. An almost perfect face. No longer young, but a face to be reckoned with. She was about forty. In fact, I knew she was exactly forty-one. Because without a doubt, without a shred of doubt, she was my cousin Clarette.

I moved back quickly, almost dropping my largest package, stepping on the toes of a man who stood behind me. "Excuse me," I mumbled, and edged closer to the wall. Although the crowd was multiplying, because the train was obviously over-due, I could still see Clarette clearly from where I stood. I felt an odd excitement and a heavy sadness. Contemplating her hair, her coat, her bag, her boots, her confident carriage, I felt a familiar irritation, which intensified as I waited and watched. I was aware that my coat was a full half inch above the hem of my skirt, that I had a run in my stocking, that my gloves were the wrong colour. Not fair, I growled to myself. Not fair. Still, burgeoning curiosity prevailed. What was she doing in To-ronto, of all places? What was she like now? Who or what had provided all that visible wealth — a legacy, a husband, a lucra-tive career? A career, I felt, would surely involve a briefcase. No millionaires lurked on the fringes of our family connection. No. It had to be a husband.

Checking my watch, I resolved to speak to her if the train should ever deign to arrive, if our seats or standing room coincided, if I could make myself do it.

❖ ❖ ❖

I am back in Lunenburg, Nova Scotia, and it is 1954. I am in my room, which has a gable overlooking the back harbour, and it is early for me to be up on a Saturday morning. But I cannot sleep. This is *the day*. I look out on the stretch of water below me, where patches of ruffled water lie isolated on the oil calm of the harbour's surface. The sun is just starting to pierce the mist, and a cloud of gulls is following a Cape Islander arriving with its morning's catch. A good omen, I feel, that today of all days should be so beautiful. It is September 15th. I am eleven years old.

It has not been a very happy September for me. My older sister, whom I adore, has left for her first year at Dalhousie. My younger brother is almost never around. And when he is, he's a king-size pest. Last week he left a dead mouse under my pillow; on Monday he stole my last package of bubble gum out of my bureau drawer. My parents are unchanged, of course, but they're old, at least forty. I might as well be an only child. I have friends I'm fond of, particularly Rosalie, my best friend. But I want a larger family. I want it to be the way it used to be.

Then, the week before, on September 8th — I will remember forever that date — my mother came to me and changed my life.

"Victoria," she said. I had always loved my name. Four syllables and regal, I felt, and prayed that no one would call me Vicky, ever. "Victoria, dear," she repeated. "I have surprising news for you. You remember your cousin Clarette? The one who came to visit us when you were six? My sister Wilma's only child. From Milwaukee. Maybe you don't remember. She was only here for two days."

I remembered. How could I forget? She had been a shot of pure crimson in our comfortable beige life. Quick and adventurous, shrieking with laughter, racing over the field to the east of the town, golden haired, a shining child — with me in eager pursuit.

"I do remember," I said.

"Well," she began, hesitating, as though I might not be too thrilled about her announcement, "Your aunt Wilma has just written to say that Clarette needs a place to stay for a while. Wilma and her husband are getting a divorce." My mother said this quickly and quietly, as though hoping I wouldn't notice. Divorces in those days were very rare indeed, and shameful — an experience that we felt happened only to Americans. Well, they were Americans, so okay. My mother continued, "Of course they're all in a state of upset. And little Clarette has been very ill. Wilma is looking for a home that is stable and healthy, where she can recover her strength."

Dared I hope? Might such a miracle happen here in Lunenburg?

"Do you think," Mother went on, still tentatively, "that you would mind sharing your room with her for a month or two? She could go to school here, and would be like a member of our own family. I'm sorry about sharing your room, but with your father using Gina's room as a study now, we have no place else to put her."

Would I mind? Would I mind having heaven deposited in my lap? I envisaged long midnight talks, deep confidences, mutual support in times of crisis. Only two weeks divided us in age. We were practically twins. And her illness intrigued and delighted me, bringing out all my mother-hen instincts. When our gang played War, I was always the nurse, wiping brows, staunching wounds, affixing splints. At eleven I still played with dolls, hugging them, cuddling them, taking them to bed, protecting them from harm. And here I was being offered a real live convalescent to care for, to watch over, to cure.

I rushed to my mother and hugged her with delight. "Oh, thank you! Thank you!" I cried.

Mother sighed with relief. "I thought you might mind," she said. "Sharing your room and all. I'll call Wilma after lunch. She'd like her to come right away, if possible. Maybe next Saturday. The fifteenth."

Moving toward the door, she turned back just once.

"Remember," she said, "it won't necessarily always be easy."

But I scarcely heard her.

❖ ❖ ❖

So I am standing by my window now, watching the morning, enfolded by its loveliness. My father has left already for the airport to meet Clarette's plane, and although it is a long drive, we can expect their arrival by early or midafternoon. I hug myself as I anticipate the prospect of her entrance into our shared room. All week long I have been tidying it, choosing the prettiest covers in the house for her bed, propping up one of my favourite dolls against her pillow. I have put a vase of goldenrod on her night table. I have helped my mother to paint her dresser — hauled down from the attic — a pale pink, to match my wallpaper, which is white, with tiny rosebuds. The curtains are of white lace, with ruffles, and there is a window seat on which my dolls sit, row on row of them. I love my room, and long to show it to Clarette.

At exactly 3:00 P.M., just as the grandfather clock is striking the hour, they arrive. I have worn my favourite dress for the occasion. It is navy blue with a tiny lace collar, and there is smocking on the yoke. Small for my age, I have long black braids with elastic bands. There are braces on my teeth and I wear glasses. I am ready and confident and very excited.

They are laughing as they come up the stairs to the verandah, my father and Clarette, and I am happy that they are already friends. My mother, I notice, is looking unreasonably nervous, but upon seeing Clarette, she relaxes, and smiles her lovely welcoming smile.

"Clarette!" she cries, rushing to her and giving her a warm hug, "How you have grown, my dear! And I see that you're as pretty as ever." She holds her out at arm's length, and then hugs her again. Then, "Clarette. I guess you remember Victoria. She certainly remembers you. She's so pleased you've come to stay with us."

Clarette does all the right things. She smiles at me with her flawless captivating smile, and says, "Thanks for letting me share your room."

She is so beautiful that my heart catches. Her hair is shoulder length with just enough, not too much, curl in it. Her eyes are cornflower blue and very intense. When she takes her coat off, I see that she has little mounds under her yellow sweater, and she is wearing jeans. She is taller than I am, and she walks like a woman. I am still excited and pleased, but I regret having got all dressed up. I wish I didn't wear glasses, because I have nice eyes, too. I am conscious of my braces when I smile at her. However, I am by nature a happy person, and my friends love me. She will, too.

"Give me your suitcase," I say, "and I'll take you upstairs."

She doesn't look one bit sick to me, but I feel she shouldn't be carrying heavy loads. She has four suitcases, all of them large, and my father carries two, while my mother and I each carry one. When they set down her bags in my room, she turns a dazzling smile upon my parents, and says, "Thanks so much, Aunt Jo and Uncle Alf. I'll try to be a perfect guest."

We all know she's going to be.

When the door closes, so does her face.

"Dolls!" she exclaims. "You don't still play with *dolls*!"

I stare, silent for a moment. But I rally quickly.

"At eleven? Goodness! Of course not! But I like to have them here for decoration. It reminds me of when I was little."

"Well," she says, face still tight shut, "my childhood doesn't happen to be something I like remembering." Then, "Where on earth am I going to put all my stuff?"

I look at the freshly painted bureau, recalling the joy in every brush stroke, and know that it will never hold the contents of those four suitcases.

"Open them up," I say, gesturing to the mountain of luggage, "and dump it all on the floor. Then we can try to figure out what to do."

I sit transfixed, watching the items come out of the luggage. Twenty-three pairs of panties, I count. Lace on most of them. Fourteen sweaters. Skirts. Slacks. Three pairs of jeans. Seven pairs of shoes. Five coats — for cool, for cold, for rain, for church. No teddy bears. Not a single doll. Some comics. Puzzle books. A picture of her mother. A picture of her father.

"She's pretty," I offer.

"Yes," she says.

"He's handsome," I add.

"Yes."

I call down to my mother. "Hey, Mom!" I yell. "We need more space for her stuff."

She comes running, and then stops, aghast, at the pile on the floor.

"I don't know what we can do," she says. "That's the last bureau in the attic. Your sister's old dresser is full of your dad's legal files, now. Oh, dear."

"No problem," I say, voice cheerful, heart somewhere near my instep. "I'll empty that big toy chest and my doll cupboard. And we can make room on the window seat. I don't play with that old stuff anymore. May as well use the space."

My mother looks at me strangely, and says, "Are you *sure*? You don't *have* to, you know. I'm sure we can think of something else." But it's obvious that she can't think of a single thing.

"Yes. I'm sure."

"Okay then, dear. That's very nice of you."

"But don't throw any of it away." I laugh lightly. "I may want to show it all to my grandchildren." Or, if she only stays for a couple of months, I can bring it all back and start where I left off.

When we finally get everything stowed away, when every available inch of the room is crammed with her belongings, we sit down on the edge of the two beds, and stare at one another.

"I'm in grade 5," I say.

"So'm I."

"We have a nice teacher this year," I tell her.

"I hate school," she says.

I love school, but dare not offer such blasphemy.

"We have art twice a week, and singing, and we do plays at Christmas time."

"Oh, whiz bang," she says, voice dreary.

"Are you still sick?" I ask her.

"No," she says.

"What did you have?"

"Don't be so nosy," she replies. "It's none of your business. I don't want to talk about it."

Foolishly, I ask, "Do you like my room?"

"Okay for a kid, I guess," she says. "But I'm used to a room of my own."

So am I. But I don't say it. The long weeks stretch ahead of me like doom.

❖ ❖ ❖

Downstairs at suppertime Clarette is all charm. *Thank you this and thank you that. How kind of you to invite me. The chicken is just delicious.* My parents are already in love with her, and I am remembering the Prodigal Son's brother.

The next day, Sunday, we all go to church. Afterwards, I take her for a walk around the town, to the beauty spots, the more important stores, the post office. I even take her high up on the western hill to show her the big wooden high school where I will be going in a few years. Brightly painted, the trim shining in the September sun, it dominates the part of the town it overlooks. It is the pride of the community.

"You mean that's a *school?*" she exclaims. "*Weird!*"

She makes various comments as we walk along.

"What dummy chose to build a town where there are so many hills?"

"Don't you ever use *brick* to build your houses?"

"What on earth do kids find to *do* in this teensy little town?"

"How come you don't have a TV? I don't know how you can *survive* without a TV."

"You mean *that* is your best friend? But she's so *fat!*" But when she was talking to Rosalie just now, she smiled her radiant smile, admired her jacket, and left a fan standing on the sidewalk.

Then she says, "How long do you have to wear all those awful braces on your teeth?"

I long to answer, And how soon will you be going home? But I reply, voice heavy, "Two more years."

"God!" she exclaims.

❖ ❖ ❖

parent/child divorce.

That night I ask her, "What are your parents like? I can't remember them. I just remember you being fun to play with." I am trying a positive approach. I don't admit defeat easily.

"They're awful," she says, "My dad must be awful, or he wouldn't have left us and run off with Mrs. Stetley. And my mom must be awful or she could have held on to him. She was always *complaining* about everything. And *criticizing*. And she shouldn't have just shipped me out, *up here*, just because she was upset." She slumps on the bed. "I hate them," she says.

Well, I can't cope with that kind of information at all. I crawl into bed, and hug Hannah, my favourite doll, whom I have hidden under my pillow. Clarette sits up and reads until eleven, flip-flipping the pages of her comic books until I want to shriek at her. Hannah is soft and comforting, minus hair, minus face — but my own, and familiar.

❖ ❖ ❖

The next day, as we get ready for school, I put on my best blue sweater, which has flowers embroidered on it. She laughs. "Are you wearing *that*?" she grins. I haul it over my flat chest, watching her as she fastens her bra over her not-very-impressive breasts. Nonetheless, they do exist, and mine do not. After a hearty breakfast prepared by my mother, to whom Clarette continues to dispense sweetness, we start off for school. Four of my friends call for me. By the time we reach school, Clarette has managed to radiate such delight, such charisma, such energy and wit that she has added four more slaves to her collection. I embrace jealousy like a lover.

❖ ❖ ❖

Clarette does not go home in two months. Divorce proceedings are held up, and Aunt Wilma writes a grateful pleading letter that effectively installs Clarette in my room for the rest of the school year. If my mother sees any connection between the four large suitcases (the twenty-three pairs of panties, for example, and the winter coat), and this turn of events, she does not speak of it. In any case, it is clear that my parents would be happy if she stayed forever. They think she is a walking angel, and she continues to act like one in their presence. I actually *visualize* her as equipped with three buttons, situated just below her collarbone. They are labelled ON, OFF, ON HOLD. They regulate The Charm. When she is with my parents and her new friends: ON! When alone with me: OFF! Then there are long periods when I see her sitting alone somewhere — in the garden, on a park bench, up in the Robertsons' tree — when she seems to have pressed the ON HOLD button. Her face is as empty as a cave, telling nothing. If my mother comes upon her when she is ON HOLD, she sometimes comes and tells me to make her snap out of it. "Go to her, Victoria," she says. "She needs you." Needs me like poison ivy, I think, but I go. I cannot tell my mother how I feel about Clarette. If I communicate my dislike for this model of kindliness and good manners, it will be I who emerge the villain. Or so I assume. Besides, tattle-taling is a crime worse than murder.

There are times when Clarette's old spell, woven so effectively at age six, wields its old power over me. She can be so funny, so fun, that I find myself loving her against my will. She thinks up marvellous games and charades, and the schoolyard sometimes comes alive with her imagination and vitality. But just when I discover that she has a toehold on my heart, she does something to destroy me a little. "Victoria," she says one day, within earshot of about thirteen of my friends, "Vic-tor-i-a," she chants. "Big old, fat old, prissy old Queen Vic-tor-i-a." Or, on the heady occasion of my coming first in the class in the Christmas exams, she announces, "Poor old dumb me, living with the Community Brain!" Or once, to my most agonizing shame, "She *sleeps* with a *doll*!" Bit by squeezing bit, she strips me of just about everything. Wallowing in self-pity, I'm tempted to suspect that she has also robbed me of my parents. But this is not so, and in my heart I sense it. Occasionally I catch my mother looking at me oddly. What is it that I see there in her eyes? Concern? Pity? Whatever it is, I sense that it is connected in some way with love, and this nourishes and sustains me.

I know, because I have been told, that Clarette will be leaving on July first. She will be going to spend the summer with her father's mother in Tennessee. And she will not return. Aunt Wilma has already enrolled her in a boarding school in New England. Although time crawls agonizingly slowly, the weeks melting into months with maddening delay, I do know that there is an end to what I am suffering. For suffering it is — let there be no mistake about it. There will be scars on my spirit at the age of forty, indelibly placed there by Clarette at the age of eleven. However, even at this time of pain, I know that I will survive. I know that when she finally leaves, I will be able to pick myself up and get on with my life — with minimal damage. That is because I am basically tough. I am a survivor, and I know it. It is true that I am a coward about some things. I am frightened of high places and fast cars, and later on, I will be afraid of subway trains. I do not have the courage to stand up to Clarette and tell her to stop tormenting me. I am afraid of her retaliations. But deep inside, I can feel something solid in the core of me, which I know will prevail. This is what keeps me going, what shelters me during these long months of invasion.

On the morning of the thirtieth of June, I wake up with an unfamiliar lightness of heart. Why? I am puzzled, and then I remember. *The last day*. I resolve to be unusually nice to Clarette. I will help her pack, will find her some little gift downtown, will smile and smile, no matter what she says or does. I do all these things, and the day passes without conflict, although it is clear that the Charm button is ON HOLD. In order to run an errand for my mother, I leave her in our room to finish packing. But she is procrastinating, sitting on the bed with one of her twenty-three pairs of panties in her hands, staring at the opposite wall. When I come back an hour later, she is lying on my bed, curled up in a ball, clutching Hannah in a savage embrace, her face wet with tears. She is asleep.

The next day, Clarette leaves with my father at nine o'clock in the morning. She will get the noon flight from Halifax International Airport, and by midnight she will be with her grandmother on her farm in Tennessee. No one comes to see her off. As her new friends have become old friends, others in grade 5 have become familiar with the OFF button. Besides, the holidays have just started, and nine o'clock is early in the morning.

When the car disappears around the corner, and I have stopped waving, I look down at the harbour, where the fog is lifting, revealing boats, reflections, beauty. I watch for a while, very still. Then I enter the house as though for the first time. The colours in the curtains, the carpet, the wallpaper, look brighter. I see the intricate pattern of the grandfather clock, which I have not noticed before. I give my mother a hug.

"Hi, Mom," I say, as though I were meeting her after a long voyage.

She holds me very close. "Hello, darling," she says. "You did well. I'm proud of you. And I think she's a lot better."

Better than what? But I have more important things to do than think about that. I am already on my way upstairs to work on my room, to return it to what it was before Clarette's tenancy.

I take warm soapy water and wash out the doll cupboard and the toy chest. I look at the extra bed and think it might be useful for pyjama parties. I decide to keep the pink bureau in case I inherit a fortune and can buy a huge new wardrobe. Then I go up to the attic to get my dolls.

There they all are — my toys, my bears, my dolls — lined up in a corner. I approach them eagerly, ready to sweep them up into my arms for their return journey to my room. But as I come closer to them, I see, to my dismay, that they have become strangers. I know with a terrible sadness that I no longer want them in my room. One or two, perhaps, for decoration. I think about dressing them, cuddling them, putting them to bed; I try to want to do it, but I feel nothing. And I deliver a parting stab of anger to Clarette for this final bitter blow. Sighing, I pick up my oldest bear and one of the dolls, and leave the attic. As I pass the full-length mirror in the hall, I catch a glimpse of myself. There are distinct little mounds under my sweater. I pass my hands over the mounds and know a kind of surprise. But that is all I sense, as I stand there alone in the upstairs hallway. Then I go into my room, close the door, and lie on my bed for a while. "Victoria," I whisper to myself, as I gaze at the ceiling. "Victoria. A lovely name."

❖ ❖ ❖

Jolted alert by the sound of the approaching train, I moved forward. Curiosity had got the better of old ghosts, and I wanted to be close enough to Clarette to speak to her. I approached obliquely from the side as the train rounded the bend, and could see that her face was in its old familiar ON HOLD position. Then, with an absence of expression of any kind, she stepped off the platform into the path of the oncoming train. No one pushed her, either on purpose or accidentally. Nor could you call it a jump. I know. I was there to see. She just walked into the air, as it were, and disappeared onto the track, at the precise moment when the train came screeching into the station. I don't remember anything more. I was somewhere else when I finally opened my eyes.

THE
REUNION

EVA HAS ONLY BEEN HERE for two hours, and already she is sorry she came. The next three days stretch ahead of her like a muddy path she will have to wade through, step by laboured step. Even with her registration completed, all events paid for — the ferry ride along the harbour, the special president's luncheon, her room and meals — she is tempted to retreat to her room and stay there, hungry but safe, for the rest of this alarming festival.

Whatever possessed her to think it would be fun? Or, as she had so naively put it, "an enriching experience, to put me in touch with my past." Had she been wholly deficient in mathematical skills? If you are going to a fifty-fifth reunion, and if you graduated at twenty-two years of age, that makes you seventy-seven. This much she knows. What she failed to do was to apply this arithmetic to everyone else. Until today, she hasn't given much thought to the ages of the other graduates. The ones in law, say, or medicine, or those erudite heroes who were pursuing graduate degrees would be much older. In fact, *old*. Or — and here she actually twitches as she stands in line outside the dining hall — *dead*. Yes, more than likely eighty-five per cent of that golden group with whom she associates such pleasure are underground, or languishing in brass or ceramic urns. Ashes. She touches her hair, her face, and runs her hand down over her hips — affirming that she is still among the living.

She looks around — up and down the tired line-up, across the familiar reception hall — and not one face does she recognize. Scrutinizing the grey hair, the bald heads, the stooped shoulders, she feels a heavy weariness pass over her. Not only is all of this depressing; suddenly it begins to seem singularly pointless. What had she intended to recapture anyway? You cannot cling to remembered laughter forever. Better, far better, to have stayed back in her room at Silver Towers, knitting, writing letters to her grandchildren, tidying her appalling bureau drawers against the threat of sickness or death.

She looks in the huge mirror across the hall. To check, she thinks wryly, on her own degree of deterioration. Well, on the whole, she feels reassured. *She* could recognize herself. A blonde once, she is now almost white, but her hair is naturally curly, and the cut, the effect, are much the same as in the past. Tiny then, and tiny now. Tinier, in fact. Osteoporosis will have its day. She grins at her own joke, and the face in the mirror comes alive — wrinkled, but undeniably *cute*.

She sighs and looks away. If only she'd realized *then* that she'd been cute. This hall, this queue, bring too many things into historical focus — too much that was far from pleasurable. Perhaps she came not so much to remember laughter as to convince herself that it had existed. So this is what I'm going to retrieve, she muses, her eyes bleak. Not only a sparse present but a diminished past. Revisited by the fears and uncertainties of being young again, she feels so weak that she moves closer to the piano (the same one?) and leans against it. The dread of academic failure, of the professors in their austere black robes; her shy discomfort in the presence of those marvellous long-legged young men; the yearnings for a different face and fuller figure; the adjusting, daily, of one's mask; the bargains she made with life. How much of that happiness she has hoped to regain was just a stale hysterical compromise with what she longed for and never had. Eva closes her eyes against the vision of such pernicious honesty. If she opens them, she will see again this hall, that furniture, those pictures, and she will be forced to examine things that should have been buried years ago.

"Are you all right?" A pretty face, an oppressively youthful face, peers down at her anxiously. Eva pushes up her bifocals and reads: "SALLY. HOSTESS."

"Thank you, my dear," says Eva, ashamed to find herself sighing again. "I was just remembering how very exhausting it was to be young. It tires me just to think about it."

"Exhausting?"

"Yes. Entirely. All those late nights. Those whispered confidences, heavy with secrets. The business of being almost constantly in love. And never knowing what to expect. Never. All that wanting that young people do. No. I don't wish ever again to be young."

The girl smiles. Obviously thinks I already have both feet firmly rooted in senility. Eva clears her throat and tries to look alert.

Sally shakes her head in disbelief. "But it's so *exciting*!"

"Exactly!" replies Eva. "You've put your finger right on it."

Sally's brows draw together, marring the perfection of that flawless forehead.

"Well," she says, "if you're quite sure you're all right . . . "

"I'm fine, Sally." Eva smiles. "Run along and embrace whatever excitement the day may offer."

Eva looks at the woman in front of her, leaning on her cane, her broad form encased in floral polyester. Behind her, a man clutches a walker. Dear heavens, she marvels, I'm a rarity. Not only alive, but upright. Free-standing.

A face is scrutinizing her. It has skin like crumpled crêpe paper, white as chalk, with two round pink spots in the absolute centre of each cheek. Her eyes, magnified and peering, look out from behind a pair of smudged glasses.

"Myra Hennigar," says the face, pointing to her own chest. "Class of '32. You won't remember me, Eva. I was a nobody back then."

We're all nobodies. Then and now.

"Hello, Myra. Of course I remember you." Indeed I do. Fat, even then. Homemade clothes, products of your mother's needle in Musquodoboit Harbour. Poor grades. Given to weeping spells.

"You haven't changed a bit, Eva."

"Nor you, Myra."

Liars. Liars, all of us. Our whole life long. Especially to ourselves.

"I always envied you, Eva. The way you seemed to have beaux by the dozen."

Beaux. What a ridiculous word. But *beau* means beautiful, male gender. Perhaps not such a bad word after all.

"Not quite by the dozen, Myra." And in the long haul, not the one I wanted. Except for those few enchanted months.

The line is moving. The doors must be opening. Sandwiched between the cane and the walker, Eva moves slowly. She looks down at her dress. Mauve silk, with a gathered skirt. Velvet choker to hide her terrible neck. *Mauve shoes.* Yes. She smiles. In spite of her neck (like the skin of a limp raw chicken), she knows she looks much better than either the walker or the cane.

But as she sits down at the table, her spirits collapse once more. That flabby person over there, gravy already running down his tie, was Buck Jamieson, football hero. *Is* Buck Jamieson. And Myra is snuggled up beside me, ready to consume me with retroactive friendship. To my right is someone who should have bought a hearing aid twenty years ago. She's from the class of '25, and of course I didn't know her then and do not care to know her now.

"Strawberry shortcake!" Eva shrieks at her. She can't read the dessert menu.

I'm sad beyond expressing, and my mauve shoes aren't helping me one bit. This table full of decrepit people depresses me, but my past drags me down even further.

"Did you marry?" This is Myra speaking. "I didn't," she adds unnecessarily, her ring finger as bare as her thumb. "Too hard to please, I guess." She giggles.

"Yes," says Eva. "I did." She finds herself sighing again. "I married Pete MacDougal. You know. He was class president in our senior year." And handsome, graduating in law, flatteringly attentive, and not at all the man I wanted to marry. Before you could turn around twice and count to twenty-five, he was markedly *in*attentive, losing his hair, and permanently infatuated with litigation, torts, real estate. And nursing an ulcer.

"How *romantic*!" breathes Myra. "I never knew you two got married. I thought you were going with someone else."

Eva lets that pass. I'm not up to discussing *that*, she thinks. She rains salt on her food, and now the meat no longer tastes like pressed sawdust. To hell with my veins and arteries. Too late anyway. Suddenly she thinks of her blood vessels as sewage pipes, clogged with sludge. She swallows quickly. "No, thank you," she says to Buck Jamieson, who is passing yet another salt cellar. "No more."

No more. No more of anything. I shall skip the boat ride; and surely I can't be expected to tour that huge athletic complex. Jazz dancing and basketball are not exactly my prime interests in life. I'll go and finish my novel in my room; maybe I'll sleep.

She sees a figure approaching from across the dining room. He walks with a cane, and he's dragging one foot.

Stroke victim, she notes. It's the one disability I haven't met today. And I'll bet you anything we'll get him at this table. Impaired speech and all.

It's a long journey, and his passage is slow. She feels a fleeting irritation that anyone in his condition would let himself be late. Making a spectacle of himself. But when he is perhaps fifty feet away, she knows who he is. Joe. Joe — still tall, masses of silver hair, and a face like a seamed granite rock. She cannot believe it, but the pulse in her neck is beating so quickly, so violently, that she's sure it must be visible. Her face feels hot, and she thinks, Can you blush at seventy-seven? The hand that holds her fork is shaking, so she puts it down and waits.

He sits directly across from her. He does not look at her name tag. "Hello, Eva," he says in his so familiar voice. His speech, thank God, thank God, is not impaired. "Where's Pete?" he asks.

"He died twenty years ago," she answers.

"I'm so sorry." He's lying, I can tell. I hope I can tell.

From Myra: "What did he die of?"

"Work," she replies with a bitterness that encases the word. But I shouldn't have married him anyway. No one should marry a person she doesn't love, just because her heart is broken.

"He did give me three wonderful children," she adds defensively. Defending whom, she wonders.

He says nothing. Nor is he eating his lunch. He is just looking, looking at her, and his expression is such that she cannot meet his eyes for very long. With her trembling fork, she pushes the peas around the plate and makes little patting motions on top of the mashed potatoes.

Finally she's able to speak again. "You were in Africa, weren't you, Joe?" Then, "How's Cynthia?" Even now, fifty-five years later, it is hard for Eva to say that name aloud. Cynthia rises up before her, bright as life, tall, with clouds of jet-black hair and violet eyes. A body like a goddess. Her *friend*. Filled with laughter, vitality and an iron will. And what she wanted, she got. Always.

"She left me after two years," he says. "She found it hot. Africa, I mean." He is still looking at Eva. "She didn't give me three wonderful children," he adds. "Even one, she felt, would ruin her figure."

Suddenly he finds he can eat. He stabs the peas with his fork, with his one good hand. He eats hungrily, and freed of his gaze, Eva discovers she can manage a few bites herself. But she knows that the maniac flutter inhabiting her midsection will play havoc with her digestion if she eats much more.

Between courses, Joe resumes his staring. By now, Eva's eyes are fixed on him, too, absorbing his signals. Someone is shouting at the deaf lady, and Buck Jamieson is dipping his napkin in his glass of water and attacking the gravy on his tie. Myra is watching Eva and Joe. The orchestra is playing songs that were popular a thousand years ago.

Finally, Joe ignores everybody and everything, and says, "Are you enjoying this awful affair, Eva?"

"No," she replies.

"Good," he says, already folding his napkin, ignoring his lemon meringue pie, which he always loved. "Let's take off. Let's go to Peggy's Cove and watch the surf. Or down to Point Pleasant Park and sit on a bench in the sun. Maybe have a double-decker ice-cream cone. Could you handle that?"

"I can handle that," says Eva, rising. She walks over to the other side of the table and takes his arm. His bad foot has very little movement, and it is slow in catching up to the other. His left arm, the one she is holding, is not doing much of anything. Eva thinks that she has never seen anyone quite as beautiful as this man. *Beau.* She is glad she wore her mauve shoes.

As she passes Sally at the door of the dining room, they smile knowingly at one another. "Are you having an exciting time, Mrs. MacDougal?" asks Sally.

"Exciting," repeats Eva. "Exactly. You've put your finger right on it."

WAITING

"YOU MUST REALIZE, OF COURSE, that Juliette is a very complex child." My mother was talking on the telephone. Shouting, to be more exact. She always spoke on the phone as though the wires had been disconnected, as though she were trying to be heard across the street through an open window. "She's so many-*sided*," she continued. "Being cute, of course, is not enough, although heaven knows she could charm the legs off a table. But you have to have something more than personality."

I was not embarrassed by any of this. Lying on the living room floor on my stomach, I was pretending to read *The Bobbsey Twins at the Seashore*. But after a while I closed the book. Letting her words drop around me, I lay there like a plant enjoying the benefit of a drenching and beneficial rain. My sister sat nearby in the huge wingback chair, legs tucked up under her, reading the funnies.

"I hope you don't regard this as *boasting*, but she really is so very, *very* talented. Bright as a button in school — three prizes, can you believe it, at the last school closing — and an outstanding athlete, even at eight years old."

Resting my head on my folded arms, I smiled quietly. I could see myself eight years from now, receiving my gold medal, while our country's flag rose in front of the Olympic flame. The applause thundered as the flag reached its peak, standing straight out from the pole, firm and strong. As the band broke into a moving rendition of "O Canada," I wept softly. I stood wet and waterlogged from my last race, my tears melding with the chlorine and coursing slowly down my face. People were murmuring, "So young, so small, and so attractive."

"And such a leader!" My mother's voice hammered on. "Even at her age, she seems forever to be president of this and director of that. I feel very blessed indeed to be the mother of such a child." My sister stirred in her chair and coughed slightly, carefully turning a page.

It was true. I was president of grade 4, and manager of the Lower Slocum Elementary School Drama Club. I had already starred in two productions, one of them a musical. In an ornate crêpe paper costume composed of giant overlapping yellow petals, I had played Lead Buttercup to a full house. Even Miss Prescott's aggressive piano playing had failed to drown me out, had not prevented me from stealing the show from the Flower Queen. My mother kept the clipping from *The Shelburne Coast Guard* up on the kitchen notice board. It included a blurred newspaper picture of me with extended arms and open mouth. Below it, the caption read, "Juliette Westhaver was the surprise star of the production, with three solos and a most sprightly little dance, performed skillfully and with gusto. Broadway, look out!"

Mama was still talking. "Mm? Oh. Henrietta. Yes, well, she's fine, I guess, just fine. Such a serious, responsible little girl, and so fond of her sister." I looked up at Henrietta, who was surveying me over the top of her comics. There was no expression on her face at all.

But then Henrietta was not often given to expression of any kind. She was my twin, but apart from the accident of our birth, or the coincidence, we had almost nothing in common. It was incredible to me that we had been born to the same parents at almost the same moment, and that we had been reared in the same house.

But Henrietta was my friend and I hers. We were, in fact, best friends, as is so often the case with twins. And as with most close childhood friendships, there was one dominant member, one submissive. There was no doubt in this case as to who played the leading role.

Henrietta even looked submissive. She was thin and pale. She had enormous sky-blue eyes surrounded by a long fringe of totally colourless eyelashes. Her hair was a dim beige colour without gradations of light or dark, and it hung straight and lifeless from two barrettes. Her fingers were long and bony, and she kept them folded in her lap, motionless, like a tired old lady. She had a straight little nose, and a mouth that seldom smiled — it was serious and still and oddly serene. She often looked as though she were waiting for something.

Untidy and flamboyant, my personality and my person flamed hotly beside her cool apathy. My temper flared, my joys exploded. With fiery red cheeks and a broad snub nose, I grinned and hooted my way through childhood, dragging and pushing Henrietta along as I raced from one adventure to the next. I had a mop of wild black curls that no comb could tame. I was small, compact, sturdy, well coordinated and extremely healthy. Henrietta had a lot of colds.

When I start talking about Henrietta and me, I always feel like I'm right back there, a kid again. Sometimes, you know, I got fed up with her. If you have a lot of energy, for instance, it's no fun to go skiing with someone who's got lead in her boots. And for heaven's sake, she kept falling all the time. Scared to death to try the hills, and likely as not going down them on the seat of her pants. "Fraidy-cat! Fraidy-cat!" I'd yell at her from the bottom of the hill where I had landed right side up, and she would start down the first part of the slope with straight and trembling knees, landing in a snowbank before the hill even got started. There were lots of fields and woods around our town, and good high hills if you were looking for thrills. You could see the sea from the top of some of them, and the wild wind up there made me feel like an explorer, a brave Indian squaw, the queen of the Maritime Provinces.

Sometimes I would let out a yell just for the joy of it all — and there, panting and gasping and falling up the hill would be old Henrietta, complaining, forever complaining, about how tired she was, how cold.

But I guess I really loved Henrietta anyway, slow-poke though she was. I had lots and lots of other friends who were more interesting than she was. But it's a funny thing — she was nearly always my first choice for someone to play with.

There was a small woodlot to the east of the village, on land owned by my father. We called it The Grove. It had little natural paths in it, and there were open spaces under the trees like rooms or houses or castles, or whatever you wanted them to be that day. The grove of trees was on the edge of a cliff overhanging some big rocks, and at high tide the sea down there was never still, even when it was flat oil calm. So it could be a spooky kind of place to play in, too. I loved to go there when it was foggy, and play Spy. It was 1940 and wartime, and by then we were ten, going on eleven. From The Grove we could sometimes see destroyers, and once even a big aircraft carrier. In the fog, it wasn't hard to believe that the Nazis were coming, and that we were going to be blown to bits any minute.

We never told Mama or Papa about going to the cliff when the mist was thick. Henrietta hardly ever wanted to go on those foggy days. She was afraid of falling off the cliff onto the rocks, sure she would drown in the churned-up water, nervous about the ghostly shapes in the thick grey-white air. But she always went. I used to blackmail her. "If you don't go, I'll tell Mama about the time you pretended to be sick and stayed home from school because you didn't have your homework done and were scared of Miss Garrison." Or I would just plain order her around. "I'm *going*, Henrietta, so get a move on and *hurry*!" She'd come padding out of the house in her stupid yellow raincoat, so that she wouldn't get a cold in the wet wind, and off we'd go — me fast and complaining about her slowness, and her slow and complaining about my speed. But she'd be there and we'd be together and we'd have fun. I'd be the Spy, and she'd be the poor agonized prisoner of war, tied up to a tree by a bunch of Nazis. Sometimes I'd leave her tethered good and long, so she'd look *really* scared instead of pretend scared, while I prowled around and killed Nazis and searched for hidden weapons. Or we'd play ghost, and I'd be the ghost — floating along on the edge of the cliff, and shrieking in my special death shriek that I saved for ghost games. It started out low like a groan, and then rose to a wail, ending in a scream so thin and high that it almost scared *me*. Sometimes, if she was especially wet and tired, Henrietta would start to cry, and that *really* made me mad. Even now, I can't stand cry babies. But you had to have a victim, and this was something she was extra good at. No point in wasting my death shriek on a person who wasn't afraid of ghosts. No fun to have the Nazis tying up someone who was big and strong and brave, particularly when the Nazis weren't actually there and you had to think them up and pretend the whole thing. One time when we went there with a bunch of kids instead of just us two, I forgot all about her being tied to the tree, and got nearly home before I raced back the whole half mile to untie her. She never said a word. It was snowing, and there were big fat snowflakes on those long white lashes of hers, and her eyes looked like they were going to pop right out of her head. I said I was real sorry, and next week I even bought her a couple of comic books out of my own allowance money, when she was home sick with bronchitis. Mama said she should have had the sense to wear a scarf and a warm hat, being as she was so prone to colds, and that's certainly true. She never told on me, and I don't know why. She sat up against the pillows and coloured in her colouring book or read her funnies, or more often she just lay there on the bed, her hands lying limp on the quilt, with that patient, quiet, waiting look of hers.

When the spring came, a gang of us would always start going out to The Grove on weekends to start practising for our summer play. Year after year we did this, and it had nothing to do with those school plays in which I made such a hit. We'd all talk about what stories we liked, and then we'd pick one of them and make a play out of it. I would usually select the play because I was always the one who directed it, so it was only fair that I'd get to do the choosing. If there was a king or a queen, I'd usually be the queen. If you're the director, you can't be something like a page or a minor fairy, because then you don't seem important enough to be giving out instructions and bossing people around, and the kids maybe won't pay attention to all the orders. Besides, as my mother pointed out, I was smart and could learn my lines fast, and you couldn't expect some slow dummy to memorize all that stuff.

Henrietta's voice was so soft and quiet that no one could ever hear her unless they were almost sitting on her lap; so of course it would have been stupid to give her a part. She couldn't even be the king's horse or the queen's milk-white mule because she was so darn scrawny. You can't have the lead animal looking as though it should be picked up by the Humane Society and put in quarantine. But she was really useful to the production, and it must have been very satisfying for her. She got to find all the costume parts, and rigged up the stage in the biggest cleared space among the trees, making it look like a ballroom or a throne room or whatever else we needed. She did a truly good job, and if it weren't for the fact that I can't stand conceited people, I probably would even have told her so. I liked Henrietta the way she was. I didn't want her strutting around looking proud of herself and putting on airs. One time one of the kids said, "Hey, Henrietta, that's a really great royal bedroom you made," and right away she started standing and moving around in a way that showed she thought she was a pretty smart stage manager.

I hate that kind of thing, and I knew the others wouldn't like it either. So I said, "Oh, sure! And the king must have just lost his kingdom in the wars. Who ever heard of a king sleeping on a pile of branches or having an old torn dishtowel at the window? Some king!" And everyone laughed. I always think that laughter is very important. It makes everyone happy right away, and is a good way to ease tensions.

We had a lot of fun practising for those plays. No one went away for the summer. No one needed to. The sea was right there alongside the village, with a big sandy beach only a quarter mile away. Some of the fishermen let us use their smaller flats for jigging, and we could always swim or dig for clams or collect mussels. Besides, the war was on; people weren't spending money on cottages or trips. Seems to me that everyone just stuck around home and saved paper and counted their ration stamps and listened to the news on the radio. There was a Navy base nearby, and sometimes sailors came to dinner. They'd tell us about life on the base, and all the dangers they were expecting and hoping to experience when they started sailing to Europe. I envied them like anything, and couldn't for the life of me see why you had to be eighteen before you joined the Navy, or why they wouldn't let girls run the ships or use the guns. Henrietta said she didn't want to be a sailor anyway, because she'd be too scared, which of course is only what you'd expect. Apart from that, there wasn't much excitement. So the play practices were our main entertainment during those years. In the summer, we practised on most fine days, and in August we put on the play in front of all our mothers and fathers and uncles and aunts, and for the sisters and brothers too young to take part.

The play we put on in 1942 was about a rich nobleman called Alphonse who falls in love with an exquisitely beautiful but humble country girl called Genevieve. I played the part of Genevieve, and it was the nicest part I had ever played. In the last scene, Genevieve and the nobleman become engaged, and she gets to dress up in a very gorgeous gown for a big court ball. I had a real dress for this scene, instead of the usual pieced-together scraps of material dug out of old trunks from our attics. My mother let me use one of her long dance dresses from when she was young. It was covered with sequins and even had some sort of fluffy feather stuff around the hem; and it was pale sapphire blue and very romantic looking. I had trouble getting into it because I was almost thirteen now and sort of big through the middle. But my mother put in a new zipper instead of the buttons, and I was able to wear it after all. I had to move a little carefully and not take very deep breaths, but I was as tall as Mama now, and I felt like a real woman, a true beauty. The neck was kind of low, but I was pretty flat, so I didn't need to worry about being indecent in front of Harold Boutilier, who played the part of Alphonse. Mama put a whole lot of makeup on me, covering up the pimples I was starting to get, and I thought I looked like a movie star, a genuine leading lady. The zipper wasn't put into the dress in time for the dress rehearsal, but Harold wore a big bow at his neck and his mother's velvet shorty coat, with a galvanized chain around his waist that shone like real silver. He had on his sister's black stockings and a pair of high rubber boots, and he looked very handsome. Up until this year he had just seemed like an okay boy to me, as boys go, but this summer I'd spent a lot of time watching him and teasing him and thinking about him when I went to bed at night. I guess I had a big crush on him. And I was pretty sure that when he saw me in that blue dress, he'd have a crush on me right away too.

On the day of the play, all our families started arriving at The Grove theatre a full hour before we got started. It didn't rain, and there wasn't even one of those noisy Nova Scotian winds that shake the trees and keep you from hearing the lines. My mother was hustling around backstage helping with clothes and makeup. Mostly she was fussing with my face and my first costume and telling me how pretty I looked. We had rigged up eight bedspreads, some torn and holey, some beautiful, depending on the fear or the pride of the mothers who lent them, and behind this strung-out curtain, we prepared ourselves for the two o'clock production. Henrietta was moving quietly about on the stage, straightening furniture, moving props, standing back to look at the effect. Later on, just before the curtain went up, or rather was drawn aside, she went off and sat down against a tree, where she'd have a good view of the performance, but where she'd be out of sight. If any of us needed anything, she could get it for us without the audience seeing what she was doing.

In the first part of the play, the nobleman ignores the beautiful peasant girl, who comes on dressed in rags but heavily made up and therefore beautiful. He is of course looking for a wife, but no one even thinks of her as a possible candidate. She does a lot of sighing and weeping, and Alphonse rides around on his horse (George Cruikshank) looking handsome and tragic. Harold did this very well. Still, I could hardly wait for the last scene in which I could get out of those rags and emerge as the radiant court butterfly. But I put all I had into this first scene, because when Alphonse turns down all the eligible and less beautiful women of the land and retires to a corner of the stage to brood (with George Cruikshank standing nearby, munching grass), Genevieve arrives on the scene to a roll of drums (our wooden spoon on Mrs. Eisner's pickling kettle). As Alphonse turns to look at her dazzling beauty, he recognizes her for what she is — not just a poor commoner, but a young woman of great charm and loveliness, worthy of his hand. At this point, she places her hand on her breast and does a deep and graceful curtsy. He stands up, bends to help her rise, and in a tender and significant gesture kisses her outstretched hand.

And that's exactly how we did it, right there on the foxberry patch, which looked like a rich green carpet with a red pattern, if you happened to have the kind of imagination to see it that way. I thought I would faint with the beauty of it all. Then the string of bedspreads was drawn across the scene, curtain hoops squeaking, and the applauding audience awaited the final scene.

I didn't waste any time getting into my other costume. Dressed in my blue gown, I peeked through the hole in Mrs. Powell's bedspread to assess the audience. I had not had time to look until now, but Mama had dressed me first, and she had six other girls to get ready for the ball scene. The crowd outside was large. There must have been forty-five or fifty people of various sizes and ages, sitting on the cushions placed on top of the pine needles. The little kids were crawling and squirming around like they always do, and mothers were passing out pacifiers and bags of chips and jelly beans and suckers to keep them quiet during intermission. One little boy — Janet Morash's brother — was crying his head off, and I sure as fire hoped he'd stop all that racket before the curtain went up. While I watched all this, I looked over to the left, and saw three sailors coming through the woods. I knew them. They'd been to our house for supper a couple of times, but I never dreamt we'd be lucky enough to have the Navy at our play. My big scene was going to be witnessed by more than just a bunch of parents and kids. There was even a little group of grade 12 boys in the back row.

We were almost ready to begin. Backstage, most of the makeup was done, and Mrs. Elliot was standing by the tree, making up Henrietta just for the heck of it. Henrietta had set up the stage and handed out the costumes, and she was putting in time like some of the rest of us. She just had on that old blue sweatshirt of hers and her dungarees, and it seemed to me that all that makeup was going to look pretty silly on someone who didn't have a costume on; but I didn't really care. If Henrietta wanted to make a fool of herself, it wasn't going to bother *me*.

In the last scene, all the courtiers and aristocrats are milling around in the ballroom, waiting for the nobleman to arrive with his betrothed. The orchestra is playing Strauss waltzes (on Mrs. Corkum's portable wind-up gramophone) and you can see that everyone is itchy footed and dying to dance, but they have to wait around until Alphonse arrives with Genevieve. It is a moment full of suspense, and I had to do a lot of smart and fierce directing to get that bunch of kids to look happy and excited and impatient all at the same time. But they did a really good job that afternoon. You could see that they thought they actually *were* lords and ladies and that it was a real live ball they had come to.

Suddenly there was a sound of trumpets (little Horace Miller's Halloween horn) and Alphonse comes in, very slow and stately, with Genevieve on his arm. She is shy, and enters with downcast eyes; but he turns around, bows to her, and she raises her head with new pride and confidence, lifting her arms to join him in the dance. We did all this beautifully, if I do say so myself, and as I started to raise my arms, I thought I would burst with the joy and splendour of that moment.

As it turned out, burst is just about exactly what I did. The waltz record was turned off during this intense scene, and there was total silence on the stage and in the audience. As my arms reached shoulder level, a sudden sound of ripping taffeta reached clear to the back of the audience. (Joannie Sherman was sitting in the last row, and she told me about it later.) I knew in one awful stupifying moment that my dress had ripped up the back, the full length of that long zipper. I can remember standing there on the stage with my arms half raised, unable to think or feel anything beyond a paralysed horror. After that night, whenever I heard that accident victims were in a state of shock, I never had to ask the meaning of that term. I knew. Joannie told me later that the whole stageful of people looked like they had been turned to stone, and that it really had been a scream to see.

Suddenly, as quiet and quick as a cat, Henrietta glided onstage. She was draped in one of the classier bedspreads from the curtain, and no one would have known that she wasn't supposed to be there. I don't know how anyone as slow-moving as Henrietta could have done so much fast thinking. But she did. She was carrying the very best bedspread — a lovely blue woven one that exactly matched my dress. She stopped in front of me, and lifting the spread with what I have to admit was a lot of ceremony and grace, she placed it gravely over my shoulders. Fastening it carefully with one of the large safety pins that she always kept attached to her sweatshirt during performances, she then moved backward two paces, and bowed first to me and then to Harold, before moving slowly and with great dignity toward the exit.

Emerging from my shock with the kind of presence of mind for which I was noted, I raised my arms and prepared to start the dance with Alphonse. But Harold, eyes full of amazement, was staring at Henrietta as she floated off the stage. From the back of the audience, I could hear two long low whistles, followed by a deep male voice exclaiming, "Hubba, *hubba*!" to which I turned and bowed in graceful acknowledgement of what I felt to be a vulgar but nonetheless sincere tribute. The low voice, not familiar to me, spoke again. "Not *you*, pie-face!" he called, and then I saw three or four of the big boys from grade 12 leave the audience and run into the woods.

Somehow or other I got through that scene. Harold pulled his enchanted eyes back onstage, and the gramophone started the first few bars of "The Blue Danube" as we began to dance. Mercifully, the scene was short, and before long we were taking our curtain calls. "Stage manager! Stage manager!" shouted one of the sailors, and after a brief pause, old Henrietta came shyly forward, bedspread gone, dressed once more in her familiar blue sweatshirt and dungarees. The applause from the audience went on and on, and as we all bowed and curtsied, I stole a look at Henrietta. Slender, I thought, throat tight. Slender, not skinny anymore. All in an instant I saw everything, right in the midst of all that clapping and bowing. It was like one of those long complicated dreams that start and finish within the space of five minutes, just before you wake up in the morning. Henrietta was standing serenely, quietly. As the clapping continued, while the actors and actresses feverishly bobbed up and down to acknowledge the applause, she just once, ever so slightly, inclined her head, gazing at the audience out of her astonishing eyes — enormous, arresting, fringed now with long dark lashes. Mrs. Elliot's makeup job had made us all see what must have been there all the time — a strikingly beautiful face. But there was something else there now that was new. As I continued to bow and smile, the word came to me to describe that strange new thing. *Power*. Henrietta had power. And what's more, she had it without having to *do* a single thing. All she needs to do, I thought, is *be*. The terrible injustice of it all stabbed me. There I was, the lead role, the director, the brains and vigour of our twinship, and suddenly, after all my years in first place, it was she who had the power. Afterwards I looked at them — the boys, the sailors, *Harold* — as they gazed at her. All she was doing was sauntering around the stage picking up props. But they were watching, and I knew, with a stunning accuracy, that there would always be watchers now, wherever she might be, whatever she wore, regardless of what she would be doing. And I also knew in that moment, with the same sureness, that I would never have that kind of power, not ever.

The next day, Mama stationed herself at the telephone, receiving all the tributes that came pouring in. A few moments per call were given over to a brief recognition of my acting talents and to an uneasy amusement over the split dress. The rest of the time was spent in shouted discussion of Henrietta's startling and surprising beauty. I lay face downward on my bed and let the words hail down upon me. "Yes, indeed. *Yes*. I quite agree. Simply beautiful. And a real bolt from the blue. She quite astonished all of us. Although of course I recognized this quality in her all along. I've often sat and contemplated her lovely eyes, her milky skin, her delicate hands, and thought, 'Your time will come, my dear! Your time will come!'"

"Delicate hands!" I whispered fiercely into the mattress. "Bony! Bony!"

I suppose, in a way, that nothing changed too drastically for me after that play. I continued to lead groups, direct shows, spark activities with my ideas, my zeal. In school I did well in all my subjects, and was good at sports, too. Henrietta's grades were mediocre, and she never even tried out for teams or anything, while I was on the swim team, the baseball team, the basketball team. She still moved slowly, languidly, as though her energy was in short supply, but there was a subtle difference in her that was hard to put your finger on. It wasn't as though she went around covered with all that highly flattering grease-paint that Mrs. Elliot had supplied. In fact, she didn't really start wearing makeup until she was fifteen or sixteen. Apparently she didn't need to. That one dramatic walk-on part with the blanket and the safety pin had done it all, although I'm sure I harboured a hope that we might return to the old Henrietta as soon as she washed her face. Even the sailors started coming to the house more often. They couldn't take her out, of course, or *do* anything with her. But they seemed to enjoy just looking at her, contemplating her. They would sit there on our big brown plush chesterfield under the stern picture of Great-great-grandmother Logan in the big gold frame, smoking cigarette after cigarette, and watching Henrietta as she moved about with her infuriatingly slow, lazy grace, her grave confidence. Her serenity soothed and excited them, all at the same time. Boys from grades 9 and 10 hung around our backyard, our verandah, the nearest street corner. They weren't mean to me. They simply didn't know I was there, not really.

I didn't spend much time with Henrietta anymore, or boss her, or make her go to The Grove in the fog or try to scare her. I just wasn't all that crazy about having her around the entire time, with those eyes looking out at me from under those long lashes, quiet, mysterious, full of power. And of course you had to trip over boys if you so much as wanted to ask her what time it was. Every once in a while I'd try to figure out what the thing was that made her so different now; and then, one day, all of a sudden, I understood. We were down at the beach, and she was just sitting on a rock or something, arms slack and resting on her knees, in a position I had often seen over the years. And in that moment I knew. Everything else was the same — the drab white skin, the bony, yes, bony hands, the limp hair. But she had lost her waiting look. Henrietta didn't look as though she were waiting for anything at all anymore.

BE-ERS
AND DOERS

Mom was a little narrow wisp of a woman. You wouldn't have thought to look at her that she could move a card table; even for me it was sometimes hard to believe the ease with which she could shove around an entire family. Often I tried to explain her to myself. She had been brought up on the South Shore of Nova Scotia. I wondered sometimes if the scenery down there had rubbed off on her — all those granite rocks and fogs and screeching gulls, the slow, labouring springs, and the quick, grudging summers. And then the winters — greyer than doom, and endless.

I was the oldest. I was around that house for five years before Maudie came along. They were peaceful, those five years, and even now it's easy to remember how everything seemed calm and simple. But now I know why. I was a conformist and malleable as early as three years old; I didn't buck the system. If Mom said, "Hurry, Adelaide!" I hurried. If she said to me, at five, "Fold that laundry, now, Adie, and don't let no grass grow under your feet," I folded it fast. So there were very few battles at first, and no major wars.

Dad, now, he was peaceful just by nature. If a tornado had come whirling in the front door and lifted the roof clear off its hinges, he probably would have just scratched the back of his neck and said, with a kind of slow surprise, "Well! Oho! Just think o' that!" He had been born in the Annapolis Valley, where the hills are round and gentle, and the summers sunlit and very warm.

"Look at your father!" Mom would say to us later. "He thinks that all he's gotta do is *be*. Well, bein' ain't good enough. You gotta *do*, too. Me, I'm a doer." All the time she was talking, she'd be knitting up a storm, or mixing dough, or pushing a mop — hands forever and ever on the move.

Although Mom was fond of pointing out to us the things our father didn't do, he must have been doing something. Our farm was in the most fertile part of the Valley, and it's true that we had the kind of soil that seemed to make things grow all of their own accord. Those beets and carrots and potatoes just came pushing up into the sunshine with an effortless grace, and they kept us well fed, with plenty left over to sell. But there was weeding and harvesting to do, and all those ten cows to milk — not to mention the fifteen apple trees in our orchard to be cared for. I think maybe he just did his work so slowly and quietly that she found it hard to believe he was doing anything at all. Besides, on the South Shore, nothing ever grew without a struggle. And when Dad was through all his chores, or in between times, he liked to just sit on our old porch swing and watch the spring unfold or the summer blossom. And in the fall, he sat there smiling, admiring the rows of vegetables, the giant sunflowers, the golden leaves gathering in the trees of North Mountain.

Maudie wasn't Maudie for the reasons a person is a Ginny or a Gertie or a Susie. She wasn't called Maudie because she was cute. She got that name because if you've got a terrible name like Maud, you have to do something to rescue it. She was called after Mom's Aunt Maud, who was a miser and had the whole Bank of Nova Scotia under her mattress. But she was a crabby old thing who just sat around living on her dead husband's stocks and bonds. A be-er, not a doer. Mom really scorned Aunt Maud and hated her name, but she had high hopes that our family would sometime cash in on that gold mine under the mattress. She hadn't counted on Aunt Maud going to Florida one winter and leaving her house in the care of a dear old friend. The dear old friend emptied the contents of the mattress, located Aunt Maud's three diamond rings, and took off for Mexico, leaving the pipes to freeze and the cat to die of starvation. After that, old Aunt Maud couldn't have cared less if everybody in the whole district had been named after her. She was that bitter.

Maudie was so like Mom that it was just as if she'd been cut out with a cookie cutter from the same dough. Raced around at top speed all through her growing-up time, full of projects and sports and hobbies and gossip and nerves. And mad at everyone who sang a different tune.

But this story's not about Maudie. I guess you could say it's mostly about Albert.

Albert was the baby. I was eight years old when he was born, and I often felt like he was my own child. He was special to all of us, I guess, except maybe to Maudie, and when Mom saw him for the first time, I watched a slow soft tenderness in her face that was a rare thing for any of us to see. I was okay because I was cooperative, and I knew she loved me. Maudie was her clone, and almost like a piece of herself, so they admired one another, although they were too similar to be at peace for very long. But Albert was something different. Right away, I knew she was going to pour into Albert something that didn't reach the rest of us, except in part. As time went on, this scared me. I could see that she'd made up her mind that Albert was going to be a perfect son. That meant, among other things, that he was going to be a fast-moving doer. And even when he was three or four, it wasn't hard for me to know that this wasn't going to be easy. Because Albert was a be-er. *Born* that way.

As the years went by, people around Wilmot used to say, "Just look at that family of Hortons. Mrs. Horton made one child — Maudie. Then there's Adelaide, who's her own self.

But Albert, now. Mr. Horton made him all by himself. They're alike as two pine needles."

And just as nice, I could have added. But Mom wasn't either pleased or amused. "You're a bad influence on that boy, Stanley," she'd say to my dad. "How's he gonna get any ambition if all he sees is a father who can spend up to an hour leanin' on his hoe, starin' at the Mountain?" Mom had it all worked out that Albert was going to be a lawyer or a doctor or a Member of Parliament.

My dad didn't argue with her, or at least not in an angry way, "Aw, c'mon now, Dorothy," he might say to her, real slow. "The vegetables are comin' along jest fine. No need to shove them more than necessary. It does a man good to look at them hills. You wanta try it sometime. They tell you things."

"Nothin' *I* need t' hear," she'd huff, and disappear into the house, clattering pans, thumping the mop, scraping the kitchen table across the floor to get at more dust. And Albert would just watch it all, saying not a word, chewing on a piece of grass.

Mom really loved my dad, even though he drove her nearly crazy. Lots more went on than just nagging and complaining. If you looked really hard, you could see that. If it hadn't been for Albert and wanting him to be a four-star son, she mightn't have bothered to make Dad look so useless. Even so, when they sat on the swing together at night, you could feel their closeness. They didn't hold hands or anything. Her hands were always too busy embroidering, crocheting, mending something, or just swatting mosquitoes. But they liked to be together. Personal chemistry, I thought as I grew older, is a mysterious and contrary thing.

One day, Albert brought his report card home from school, and Mom looked at it hard and anxious, eyebrows knotted. "'Albert seems a nice child,'" she read aloud to all of us, more loudly than necessary, "'but his marks could be better. He spends too much time looking out the window, dreaming.'" She paused. No one spoke.

"Leanin' on his hoe," continued Mom testily. "Albert!" she snapped at him. "You pull up your socks by Easter or you're gonna be in deep trouble."

Dad stirred uneasily in his chair. "Aw, Dorothy," he mumbled. "Leave him be. He's a good kid."

"Or could be. *Maybe*," she threw back at him. "What he seems like to me is rock-bottom lazy. He sure is slow-moving, and could be he's slow in the head, too. Dumb."

Albert's eyes flickered at that word, but that's all. He just stood there and watched, eyes level.

"But I love him a lot," continued Mom, "and unlike you, I don't plan t' just sit around and watch him grow dumber. If it's the last thing I do, I'm gonna light a fire under his feet."

Albert was twelve then, and the nagging began to accelerate in earnest.

"How come you got a low mark in your math test?"

"I don't like math. It seems like my head don't want it."

"But do you *work* at it?"

"Well, no. Not much. Can't see no sense in workin' hard at something I'll never use. I can add up our grocery bill. I pass. That's enough."

"Not for me, it ain't," she'd storm back at him. "No baseball practice for you until you get them sums perfect. Ask Maudie t' check them." Maudie used to drum that arithmetic into him night after night. She loved playing schoolteacher, and that's how she eventually ended up. And a cross one.

One thing Albert was good at, though, was English class. By the time he got to high school, he spent almost as much time reading as he did staring into space. His way of speaking changed. He stopped dropping his g's. He said *isn't* instead of *ain't*. His tenses were all neated up. He wasn't putting on airs. I just think that all those people in his books started being more real to him than his own neighbours. He loved animals, too. He made friends with the calves and even the cows. Mutt and Jeff, our two grey cats, slept on his bed every night. Often you could see him out in the fields, talking to our dog, while he was working.

"Always messin' around with animals," complained Mom. "Sometimes I think he's three parts woman and one part child. He's fifteen years old, and last week I caught him bawlin' in the hayloft after we had to shoot that male calf. Couldn't understand why y' can't go on feedin' an animal that'll never produce milk."

"Nothing wrong with liking animals," I argued. I was home for the weekend from my secretarial job in Wolfville.

"Talkin' to dogs and cryin' over cattle is not what I'd call a short cut to success. And the cats spend so much time with him that they've forgotten why we brought them into the house in the first place. For mice."

"Maybe there's more to life than success or mice," I said. I was twenty-three now, and more interested in Albert than in conformity.

Mom made a "huh" sound through her nose. "Adelaide Horton," she said, "when you're my age, you'll understand more about success and mice than you do now. Or the lack of them." She turned on her heel and went back in the house. "And if you can't see," she said through the screen door, "why I don't want Albert to end up exactly like your father, then you've got even less sense than I thought you had. I don't want any son of mine goin' through life just satisfied to *be*." Then I could hear her banging around out in the kitchen.

I looked off the verandah out at the front field, where Dad and Albert were raking up hay for the cattle, slowly, with lots of pauses for talk. All of a sudden they stopped, and Albert pointed up to the sky. It was fall, and four long wedges of geese were flying far above us, casting down their strange muffled cry. The sky was cornflower blue, and the wind was sending white clouds scudding across it. My breath was caught with the beauty of it all, and as I looked at Dad and Albert, they threw away their rakes and lay down flat on their backs, right there in the front pasture, in order to drink in the sky. And after all the geese had passed over, they stayed like that for maybe twenty minutes more.

❖ ❖ ❖

We were all home for Christmas the year Albert turned eighteen. Maudie was having her Christmas break from teaching, and she was looking skinnier and more tight-lipped than I remembered her. I was there with my husband and my new baby, Jennifer, and Albert was even quieter than usual. But content, I thought. Not making any waves. Mom had intensified her big campaign to have him go to Acadia University in the fall. "Pre-law," she said, "or maybe teacher training. Anyways, you gotta go. A man has to be successful." She avoided my father's eyes. "In the fall," she said. "For sure."

"It's Christmas," said Dad, without anger. "Let's just be happy and forget all them plans for a few days." He was sitting at the kitchen table breaking up the bread slowly, slowly, for the turkey stuffing. He chuckled. "I've decided to be a doer this Christmas."

"And if the doin's bein' done at that speed," she said, taking the bowl from him, "we'll be eatin' Christmas dinner on New Year's Day." She started to break up the bread so quickly that you could hardly focus on her flying fingers.

Christmas came and went. It was a pleasant time. The food was good; Jennifer slept right through dinner and didn't cry all day. We listened to the Queen's Christmas message; we opened presents. Dad gave Mom a ring with a tiny sapphire in it, although she'd asked for a new vacuum cleaner.

"I like this better," she said, and looked as though she might cry.

"We'll get the vacuum cleaner in January," he said, "That's no kind of gift to get for Christmas. It's a work thing."

She looked as if she might say something, but she didn't.

❖ ❖ ❖

It was Boxing Day when it happened. That was the day of the fire.

It was a lazy day. We all got up late, except me, of course, who had to feed the baby at two and at six. But when we were all up, we just sort of lazed around in our dressing gowns, drinking coffee, admiring one anothers' presents, talking about old times, singing a carol or two around the old organ. Dad had that look on him that he used to get when all his children were in his house at the same time. Like he was in temporary possession of the best that life had to offer. Even Mom was softened up, and she sat by the grate fire and talked a bit, although there was still a lot of jumping up and down and rushing out to the kitchen to check the stove or cut up vegetables. Me, I think on Boxing Day you should just eat up leftovers and enjoy a slow state of collapse. But you can't blame a person for feeding you. It's handy to have a Martha or two around a house that's already equipped with three Marys. Albert was the best one to watch, though. To me, anyway. He was sitting on the floor in his striped pajamas, holding Jennifer, rocking her, and singing songs to her in a low, crooning voice. Tender, I thought, the way I like a man to be.

Albert had just put the baby back in her carriage when a giant spark flew out of the fireplace. It hit the old nylon carpet like an incendiary bomb, and the rug burst into flames. Mom started waving an old afghan over it, as though she was blowing out a match, but all she was doing was fanning the fire.

While most of us stood there in immovable fear, Albert had already grabbed Jennifer, carriage and all, and rushed out to the barn with her. He was back in a flash, just in time to see Maudie's dressing gown catch fire. He pushed her down on the floor and lay on top of her and smothered the flames, and then he was up on his feet again, taking charge.

"Those four buckets in the summer kitchen!" he yelled. "Start filling them!" He pointed to Mom and Dad, who obeyed him like he was a general and they were the privates. To my husband he roared, "Get out to th' barn and keep that baby warm!"

"And you!" He pointed at me. "Call the fire department. It's 825-3131." In the meantime, the smoke was starting to fill the room and we were all coughing. Little spits of fire were crawling up the curtains, and Maudie was just standing there, shrieking.

Before Mom and Dad got back with the water, Albert was out in the back bedroom hauling up the carpet. Racing in with it over his shoulder, he bellowed, "Get out o' the way!" and we all moved. Then he slapped the carpet over the flames on the floor, and the fire just died without so much as a protest. Next he grabbed one of the big cushions off the sofa, and chased around after the little lapping flames on curtains and chairs and table runners, smothering them. When Mom and Dad appeared with a bucket in each hand, he shouted,

"Stop! Don't use that stuff! No need t' have water damage too!"

Then Albert was suddenly still, hands hanging at his sides with the fingers spread. He smiled shyly.

"It's out," he said.

I rushed up and hugged him, wailing like a baby, loving him, thanking him. For protecting Jennifer — from smoke, from fire, from cold, from heaven knows what. Everyone opened windows and doors, and before too long, even the smoke was gone. It smelled pretty awful, but no one cared.

When we all gathered again in the parlour to clear up the mess, and Jennifer was back in my bedroom asleep, Mom stood up and looked at Albert, her eyes ablaze with admiration — and with something else I couldn't put my finger on.

"Albert!" she breathed, "We all thank you! You've saved the house, the baby, all of us, even our Christmas presents. I'm proud, proud, *proud* of you."

Albert just stood there, smiling quietly, but very pale. His hands were getting red and sort of puckered looking.

Mom took a deep breath. "And *that*," she went on, "is what I've been looking for, all of your life. Some sort of a sign that you were one hundred per cent alive. And now we all know you are. Maybe even a lick more alive than the rest of us. So!" She folded her arms, and her eyes bored into him. "I'll have no more excuses from you now. No one who can put out a house fire single-handed and rescue a niece and a sister and organize us all into a fire brigade is gonna sit around for the rest of his life gatherin' dust. No siree! Or leanin' against no hoe. Why, you even had the fire department number tucked away in your head. Just imagine what you're gonna be able to do with them kind o' brains! I'll never, never rest until I see you educated and successful. Doin' what you was meant to do. I'm just proud of you, Albert. So terrible proud!"

Members of the fire department were starting to arrive at the front door, but Albert ignored them. He was white now, like death, and he made a low and terrible sound. He didn't exactly pull his lips back from his teeth and growl, but the result was similar. It was like the sound a dog makes before he leaps for the throat. And what he said was *"You jest leave me be, woman!"*

We'd never heard words like this coming out of Albert, and the parlour was as still as night as we all listened.

"You ain't proud o' me, Mom," he whispered, all his beautiful grammar gone. "Yer jest proud o' what you want me t' be. And I got some news for you. Things I shoulda tole you years gone by. *I ain't gonna be what you want.*" His voice was starting to quaver now, and he was trembling all over. "*I'm gonna be me.* And it seems like if that's ever gonna happen, it'll have t' be in some other place. And I plan t' do somethin' about that before the day is out."

Then he shut his eyes and fainted right down onto the charred carpet. The firemen carted him off to the hospital, where he was treated for shock and second-degree burns. He was there for three weeks.

❖ ❖ ❖

My dad died of a stroke when he was sixty-six. "Not enough exercise," said Mom, after she'd got over the worst part of her grief. "Too much sittin' around watchin' the lilacs grow. No way for his blood to circulate good." Me, I ask myself if he just piled up his silent tensions until he burst wide open. Maybe he wasn't all that calm and peaceful after all. Could be he was just waiting, like Albert, for the moment when it would all come pouring out. Perhaps that wasn't the way it was; but all the same, I wonder.

Mom's still going strong at eighty-eight. Unlike Dad's, her blood must circulate like a racing stream, what with all that rushing around; she continues to move as if she's being chased. She's still knitting and preserving and scrubbing and mending and preaching. She'll never get one of those tension diseases like angina or cancer or even arthritis, because she doesn't keep one single thing bottled up inside her for more than five minutes. Out it all comes like air out of a flat tire — with either a hiss or a bang.

Perhaps it wasn't growing up on the South Shore that made Mom the way she is. I live on that coast now, and I've learned that it's more than just grey and stormy. I know about the long sandy beaches and the peace that comes of a clear horizon. I've seen the razzle-dazzle colours of the low-lying scarlet bushes in the fall, blazing against the black of the spruce trees and the bluest sky in the world. I'm familiar with the way one single radiant summer day can make you forget a whole fortnight of fog — like birth after a long labour. You might say that the breakers out on the reefs are angry or full of threats. To me, though, those waves are leaping and dancing, wild with freedom and joyfulness. But I think Mom was in a hurry from the moment she was born. I doubt if she ever stopped long enough to take notice of things like that.

Albert left home as soon as he got out of the hospital. He worked as a stevedore in Halifax for a number of years, and when he got enough money saved, he bought a little run-down house close to Digby, with a view of the Bay of Fundy. He's got a small chunk of land that's so black and rich that it doesn't take any pushing at all to make the flowers and vegetables grow. He has a cow and a beagle and four cats — and about five hundred books. He fixes lawn mowers and boat engines for the people in his area, and he putters away at his funny little house. He writes pieces for *The Digby Courier*, and *The Novascotian*, and last winter he confessed to me that he writes poetry. He's childless and wifeless, but he has the time of day for any kid who comes around to hear stories or to have a broken toy fixed. He keeps an old rocker out on the edge of the cliff, where he can sit and watch the tides of Fundy rise and fall.

THE PEN PAL

23 Howe St.,
Lunenburg, Nova Scotia,
Canada
April 9, 1983

Dear Hilary:

I have chosen you as my pen pal for two reasons. The first is because of your name. I had a best friend in grade 3 who was called Hilary. She moved away to Montreal in grade 4, and I have never again had a friend quite so loyal and true. I also love the name. It is full of subtle rhythms. *Hi*-lary. *Hi*-lary. *Tum*-tee-tee. *Tum*-tee-tee. I wish I had a name like that. My name is Edna.

The second reason I have chosen you is that you are so many miles away. I have looked at the map very carefully, and I can see that Australia is as far off as it is possible to be, unless you walk right off the edge of the earth into outer space. But I don't believe that will be necessary. I don't think that any secrets I tell an Australian are ever going to come back to haunt me in Nova Scotia, Canada.

Our teacher gave us a list of pen pals last Thursday in our English composition class. She is a great believer in communication, and we were all urged to choose a name. She did not need to urge me at all. I need a pen pal the way some people need water or oxygen. I am so full of miseries and raptures that I think I may explode if I don't let some of them out. Thirteen seems to be a very bursting time of life. But you have to be exceedingly careful to whom you do your erupting. No doubt you have discovered this yourself, being thirteen and a half as of last Friday. I hope you will not be put off by the fact that I am only just thirteen. People who know me well say that I am very old for my age, and have an unusually mature vocabulary.

But I will have to admit that I feel retarded in a number of other ways. Up until two weeks ago I was twelve, and I now find the idea of being twelve repugnant to me. A person that age is just barely formed inside and out. At twelve you have what the novelists call "budding breasts," which simply means that you have little mounds or sort of giant pimples, which won't fit into any bras manufactured by anyone in the world. When I grow to be really old, in my thirties maybe, I'm going to make my fortune by inventing a brassiere that won't wrinkle when placed over a budding breast. Because you are thirteen and a half, you are probably fully formed. I have a long way to go. This is very annoying, because my hips have suddenly grown wide enough to accommodate triplets. This hardly seems fair. I want to look like an hourglass, not a pear.

When twelve, I was also very unformed inside. But by the evening of my thirteenth birthday, I could already feel a great difference. I could sense that the child part of me was receding, and that a marvellous woman was about to emerge, like a genie out of a bottle. I have a number of sophisticated friends who acted daring and confident at eleven, but I seem to have been slow in moving into this phase. This has been a hard adjustment for me, because as a young child, I was always at the top of the heap, a great leader. But as soon as this woman thing got started in all of us, I felt as if I was bringing up the rear on crutches. A large vocabulary is of no use whatsoever at such times. Don't let anyone tell you that verbal skills are more important than physical ones.

I hope you will be very frank with me. I myself will tell all. My mind is teeming with succulent confidences that I long to share. But I know if I told even one of these to my very best friend, Catherine, the whole school would be lapping it up within twenty-four hours. If I told it to anyone else, the time lag would be more like forty-five minutes. Sometimes I wonder if you can trust anybody. That's why I chose a pen pal from Australia.

This is going to be a very long letter, but if an introduction is to be significant, it has to take up more than half a page. Here are some facts about me. Then I'll wait and see what kind of person you are before I spill all my secrets into your lap.

I am of medium height and I have naturally curly brown hair. This means it's frizzy when long, quite nice when short, and can never, never be straight and gleaming and glossy like the Breck Girl advertisements. I have a good nose and large blue eyes — quite acceptable, really. But I'm shortsighted. I wear glasses — big thick ones. Just my luck.

I have a ten-year-old brother, Hugo, who I like (*whom* I like) quite a lot. But boys of that age are certainly 100% boys, which may or may not be desirable. I like men to be strong and brave, but it would be nice if once in a while they could also be gentle and considerate. My father is good at this, but Hugo has no time for that kind of thing. He is forever playing hockey in the winter (your summer) or baseball in the spring, and is eternally flexing his muscles in front of the hall mirror. He loves jumping out from behind closed doors to scare you, and I just hope I don't have a heart attack before I turn eighteen. Hugo is always *doing* something — and never seems to *think* about anything. But there may be things going on in his head that I don't know about. Mostly he is a pest, but if he was drowning, I would certainly feel obliged to rescue him.

My mother is extremely young. Girls who have grey-haired

mothers in their forties envy me. She looks like my older sister. She told me that she had her children young so that she could share her youth with them and enjoy them. But she has a very time-consuming job, which she says fulfills her. This means she doesn't have to share her youth or anything else with Hugo or me, or even with my dad — although significant things may go on behind that closed bedroom door in the dead of night. I'm not blaming her for being forever busy. It's really a tight squeeze to cram all the rest of her day into the hours between six and midnight. All the shopping and cooking and washing and stuff. I help her some, although maybe not enough. But it wasn't *me* that chose to have her work at that fulfilling job of hers. It was her. And Hugo, of course, never lifts a finger. Mother is a great feminist and women's lib person and joins all their groups and signs petitions and things. But I notice she never asks Hugo to dry the dishes. This really bugs me.

My mother came from "an old Halifax family." In her case, that meant her father was an admiral. With other people it can mean politics or beer. But beware of old Halifax families. Most of them are really deluded. They are very Junior League and Harris tweed, and think that the blood coursing through their veins is different from everybody else's. Mother once had to have a blood transfusion after a miscarriage. I wonder how she felt, knowing that some stranger's blood was entering her body — and *saving her life*. It could have been a prostitute's or a junkie's. Or Jeffrey's. He's one of the truck drivers from Eisenhauer's Seafoods. I know his name is Jeffrey, because Catherine and I used to sneak rides on his truck with him when we were little kids. He chewed tobacco and spat all the time — sometimes not too accurately — but apart from that, we liked him a lot. He loved to tell us shocking things about people in the town. And of course we loved to listen. He told us about some of the amazing things that went on down by the water-front at night — deliciously embarrassing things. He also described the people who went out and took usable fish parts off the wharves, even stealing knives that the men left lying around — and you wouldn't believe who some of those people were. But we couldn't ever tell anyone, because then everybody would have wanted to know how we found out. My mother would have killed me and cut me up in little pieces if she'd ever found out about our trips in that truck. It was the one secret that Catherine was able to keep forever.

I think I'll stop now. I guess maybe I'll write again before your letter comes. It will probably take a million years for mail to travel so far, and I don't think I can wait that long. I have too many things craving to be expressed.

> Yours sincerely,
> Your Canadian friend,
> Edna Publicover

❖ ❖ ❖

> 23 Howe St., Et cetera
> April 16, 1983

Dear Hilary:

I have sent your first letter, and now I'm writing a second. But not as much as the last time.

I'd like to tell you about my father. He has a good job at Whynacht and Company Limited. He manages things. He's an engineer with all kinds of brains, and he's over six feet tall, and looks like he should be playing one of the lead roles on "The Young and The Restless." But his father was a *blue-collar worker*, and this is like a scar in the dead centre of my father's face. If you want to know what tension is like, come over and visit us some Christmas. When people hear carols being sung, most people get all mushy inside, and tears come to their eyes

as they remember happy family scenes before the blazing yule
log, tree-trimming on Christmas Eve, candles and music in
church, the magic of the Christmas story. When I hear those
Christmas songs, my stomach squeezes up like a fist as I recall
our yearly meetings between the two families. My mother's
father wears pinstriped trousers at Christmas, and always turns
up in spats. Did you read what I said? *Spats*. Her mother is
courteous and controlled, and looks as though she swallowed
a poker. My dad's folks are really nice, but even I who love
them can see that they are all *wrong*. It isn't just what they look
like — Grandpa Publicover's too-short sleeves on his jacket
and his red wrists with no shirt cuffs showing, and Gramma
Publicover's flowered dresses. There's something a whole lot
worse. They speak with bad grammar. There are no "ain'ts,"
but there are a lot of "she don'ts" and "they wasn'ts." Everyone
pretends so hard not to notice that the tension is almost visible
in the air. In fact, it *is* visible. My mother, who is normally very
quiet and self-contained, goes flapping around readjusting the
ornaments on the piano, and talking with an oppressive kind
of gaiety. Daddy, who is usually so soft and laughing and
easygoing, becomes very silent, and although he is always
polite to his parents, there is a curtain over his eyes that is
normally not there. I really much prefer my wrong grandparents to my right ones, and it is very difficult not to let this show.
In fact, just about everything is difficult. On Boxing Day, after
they leave, everyone is irritable from all that strain. We eat cold
turkey and snap at one another. I wish we could have the
grandparents year and year about. But Mother says that because she and Daddy were each an only child, there'd be
nowhere for either couple to go if they took turns. And she
says that it would be very uncharitable to neglect them at
Christmastime. If it were me, I'd rather be very happy every
second year, and put up with a little misery in the off-
Christmases. I told this to Mother, but she said I'd understand

better when I got older. They're always saying this. It doesn't solve a blessed thing.

This turned out to be longer than I intended. I am discovering that having a pen pal is very time-consuming, but also very purgative. I mean this, of course, in the psychological sense of the word.

I will die of excitement the first time I get one of your letters.

> Affectionately,
> Your friend from across
> the Seas,
> Edna

❖ ❖ ❖

> Lunenburg, April 20

Dear Hilary:

I am writing to warn you to send all your letters by airmail. I sent your first two by "surface mail." This is such a romantic term, but so slow. One envisions one's letter moving languidly over slimy southern seas, or tossed back and forth across the hold (in waterproof bags, one hopes) during terrible storms, which I prefer to think of as tempests if they happen at sea.

I had the most terrible, truly *terrible* thing happen to me today. I am deeply in love with Johnny Maloney. I think I have not mentioned this to you before. How could I not have told you? But what is there to tell? Nothing ever happens worth telling. Except for the roiling, whirling white-hot state of my heart within me. That is worth telling about. I have daydreams about him that would set you aflame if I were to tell you the details. But he is sixteen, and seems not to have noticed that I am now thirteen. Nor that my soul is a great deal more attractive than my body. Nor that I have naturally curly hair. In my daydreams, I do not look like a pear, and my hips have sort of peeled away to a soft curve. I also wear V-necked sweaters in order to do justice to my considerable cleavage. Most of my dreams start with the same scene: I am standing in a large group of happy people, probably at a party. There is a pause in the conversation, and I turn casually to discover that Johnny is standing there staring at me as though I were an apparition. Finally, when he can manage to speak, he says, "Edna!" (in a choked voice). "How could I have failed to notice you before?" I'll tell you how. Because the apparition bears not the slightest resemblance to the reality.

I was about to tell you about my moment of abysmal suffering today. My mother had given me a list of things she wanted at the drugstore, and I went to pick them up after school. Can you believe this list? Four rolls of toilet paper, one large bottle of Bromo Seltzer, three (three!) bottles of Metamucil, a package of pocket-size Eno and some Q-tips. Not one item is what you could call respectable. The Q-tips come closest, but anyone with a little imagination knows that they are used for digging out either your ears or your nose. I was holding all these things in my arms, because I had forgotten to pick up a wire basket, and who should be standing at the cash register but Johnny Maloney. He turned and smiled at me and said, "Hi, Edna." You will notice that he didn't say, "How could I have failed to notice you before?" But in ordinary circumstances I would have been thrilled by "Hi, Edna." That's one of the things that made me plunge so deeply in love with him in the first place. He smiles at everybody and remembers names. He will do well in politics when he is older, or the diplomatic service. Or maybe just as the father of some incredibly lucky child, or the husband of someone who is smart enough to know how fortunate she is. Like, oh dear sweet heavens, *me*.

Anyway, there he is standing there, and he follows up his "Hi, Edna" with "How are things?" He has his stuff paid for by now (probably chocolate bars or hair spray for his mother, or a magazine — unembarrassing things), and comes over and waits for my answer. I can feel myself fiery hot and red in the face, and I say, "Great, thanks. How's life with you?" Then, while I stand there willing instant death, the Bromo Seltzer goes crashing to the ground, and he of course picks it up for me. He lays it carefully on top of the mountain of merchandise that I am hugging — on top of the Eno, the toilet paper, the *three* bottles of Metamucil, the Q-tips. His eyes keep coming back to my armload of shame, but he does not offer to carry any of it for me. There are some things that no one will offer to carry, especially for someone who is shaped like a pear. I wanted him to leave so badly that for a few moments I almost hated him. But he stayed and stayed, and the cashier kept waiting for me to put all the stuff on the counter. Which I was not about to do, supposing my arms fell right out at the roots. It crossed my mind to say that none of these things was for me, or that I was picking up some items for my mother. But my mother looks so perfect that no one would ever believe that she kept a stomach or a bowel inside those immaculate clothes, let along malfunctioning ones. After what seemed like twenty-four hours, he said, "Well, see ya around," and left.

When I got home, I almost threw the package at my mother, and stomped upstairs. "Adolescence!" sighed Mother to my dad. "Always gloomy about *something*. I wouldn't be that age again for a million dollars." Now that, I thought, is the first wise thing I've heard from her for months.

Do things like that ever happen to you? I'll not be able to bear it if you are prematurely gorgeous, and equipped with an unnatural poise, sailing through life on top of the wave.

Yours till the kitchen sinks,
Edna

P.S. Please send a picture of yourself. I enclose the only one of me that I can find. My father took it with a telephoto lens. I'm on the very top of a ferris wheel. The reason my mouth is open is that I was scared out of my wits. However, you can see my curly hair, and my hips are nowhere in sight.

❖ ❖ ❖

23 Howe St., Lunenburg
Nova Scotia, Canada
April 25, 1983

Dear Hilary:

Today I got my period for the very first time. I suppose you got yours at eleven or twelve, like everyone else in the world, altho' I know a girl in grade 10 who is *still waiting*. I was greatly relieved at first, to know at long last that I was a 100% normal woman. That was at 7:30 in the morning. I was all prepared, of course, and knew what to do about everything. My mother had given me all sorts of *clinical* instructions five years ago, and it was the hottest topic of conversation among my friends in Grade 6. Thank heavens it was Saturday. By noon I was thinking, If this is the only alternative, who wants it? By six o'clock, I was hating every boy, every man in the entire universe, because they are *spared*. "Unfair, unfair!" I muttered through my teeth, as I locked myself in the bathroom to cope with the *equipment*. Then my mother kept knocking on the door and saying, with rising irritation, "Edna! Hurry up! Dinner has been ready for ten minutes. Your father is *hungry*." I didn't care if my father stayed hungry for the rest of his life, or if he starved to death with a distended belly, like in the pictures I had seen of people suffering from famine. Hunger was a small problem to cope with compared to *this*. I wanted to scream and scream, "Leave me alone!"

Now it is late at night, and I am so depressed. My whole life stretches before me without help or hope, marked off in sections of four week intervals. Three weeks good. One week bad. Forever. Until I'm pregnant or old. I cannot imagine a God who would devise such a system for regularizing the reproductive process. Ever since I was six, I have felt scorn for anyone who believed that the stork brought babies. Now I can see that it is a wonderful idea. So tidy and simple and clean. But if this is the only alternative, I'm not very crazy about it.

Then I remembered Marilyn Jocassi, who always has terrible cramps. I recalled a day when she was all doubled up on the floor of the girls' washroom, rocking back and forth, white as paper. Sylvia Buchanan looked down at her as though she were a *thing*, and said in oh so cold a voice, "Cramps! What a fuss-pot. All in her mind." Marilyn stopped rocking for a moment and glared at Sylvia with such a look of hatred that it frightened me to see it. I guess hate is something we all feel from time to time, but it is a shock to see it come pouring out of a pair of eyes like that.

Maybe you think I'm childish to mind this so much. I told my mother how I felt, and she smiled and patted me on the shoulder. "You'll get used to it," she said. "Believe me. You will." Get used to it. Like people get used to false teeth and bald heads and pimples and migraine headaches and suffering from unrequited love.

> Yours in depths of gloom,
> Edna

P.S. Edna is such a horrible name. The admiral's wife is called Edna. My Publicover grandmother's name is Sadie, and that's my middle name. Not much to choose from.

❖　❖　❖

Lunenburg, April 27

Dear Hilary:

I wish a letter from you would hurry up and come. I really need someone to let off steam to. Last night I wanted so badly to have a really long talk with Mother about my period. She was nice and kind and everything, but she just had no *time*. And she really didn't. She had a meeting to prepare for the following day at work, four loads of washing to do, and the weekly letters to write to the grandparents. I started to fold the laundry for her, thinking we could talk while we worked together. But she said, "Oh, good! Thank you darling. Now I'm free to go and work on that agenda," and kissed me on the top of my head and left. I wanted to ask her what you do on *picnics*, for heaven's sake, or on a *camping trip*. But that isn't my real problem. The whole business is so mysterious that maybe I couldn't have discussed it anyway. Because I'm not even sure what it is. It's an awful feeling of something being gone that I will never have again. And of having come face to face with something else I cannot even recognize, let alone cope with.

Love,
Edna

❖　❖　❖

Lunenburg, May 6

Dear Hilary:

Today was such a wonderful day. I thought I would collapse

from the delight of it all. The morning was unusually warm for early May, and I kicked off my Adidas and socks and ran and ran over the fields overlooking the Back Harbour. Nova Scotia is a bit like me, I think. There's a lot of fog and rain and raw winds. But when the sun shines on the sea, the joy can be almost unbearable.

Here are some other reasons for happiness today:

1.   Johnny Maloney smiled at me, on the corner of Lincoln and King, when I went to pick up the mail. He also spoke. He said, "How's life, Edna?"

2.   My mother was home with a bad cold. I love it when she's sick. I bring her hot drinks on trays and plump up her pillows. Then I sit down on the edge of her bed and talk. She is a good listener when she has enough time.

3.   I saw a really cute little baby today, sitting up in a carriage, outside *The Progress Enterprise* office. I said to myself, I could have one of those, anytime I wanted. The thought was amazing. I went cold and hot and goosebumps all over. "*Men can't do it!*" I whispered to myself, right there on Montague St. I felt sorry for men, and quite arrogant. I was proud to be me.

> Write soon.
> From your friend, who is
> tired of holding a one-way
> conversation,
> Edna

❖ ❖ ❖

May 15

Hilary — If I don't hear from you by June 1st, I'm going to stop writing. It would be just as easy to write in a diary, and a lot less expensive.

The Admiral came to visit us today from Halifax. Even my

mother calls him the Admiral, although he has been retired for
five years. She says that he always expected her and her mother
to act like the Ratings. Yes sir, no sir, very good sir. And
everyone knows that no Admiral communicates, *really* communicates, with a Rating. There are no Ratings now, but in
my grandfather's heyday, the Navy was really the Navy, and
the boys who wore the cute sailor suits were the Ratings. But
they were rock bottom on the scale of things, and that's often
how Mother and Grandma felt. It is nice when parents tell you
things like this, and kind of surprising. It is hard to think of a
mother as being anything but a mother. The Admiral said to
me, "Go get my suitcase out of the car." Ordered, not asked.
I'm going to shock him some day by saluting. Or by saying,
"You may think you know everything on the sea and on dry
land, but my body is more remarkable than yours. All you can
do is plant a silly old seed. I am fully and most intricately
equipped to turn a seed into a whole live baby." Imagine his
face if I said that. And I bet if I said the same kind of thing to
my other grandfather, he'd bellow with laughter and say,
"More power to ya, kid!" No matter how hard I try, I can't
imagine the Admiral planting the seed. Nor, for that matter,
the Admiral's wife receiving it.

> What are your grand-
> parents like?
> Your friend,
> Edna

P.S. If your first letter ever does arrive, I may be too excited to
open it.

❖ ❖ ❖

23 Howe St.,
Lunenburg, Nova Scotia,
Canada
May 23, 1983

Dear Hilary:

I have received your letter. I am of course humiliated beyond belief. They should make it clear on those pen-pal lists whether a person is a girl or a boy. I did not know that Hilary could be a boy's name.

Please be good enough to take all my letters and burn them. I do not like to think of the things I may have written.

Yours sincerely,
Edna Publicover

P.S. If any of my letters have been held up and are delivered after the arrival of this one, please throw them away unopened. Better still, shred them.

P.P.S. Please do not write to me again.

E.P.